The 13th Chair Presents

BAND = LIFE

An omnibus of the **BAND NERDS** book series.

Written By
DJ Corchin

Illustrated By
Dan Dougherty

The phazelFOZ Company, LLC

BAND=LIFE
Copyright © 2017 By The phazelFOZ Company, LLC.

All rights reserved. No part of this book may be reproduced or transmitted in any form or by any means, electronic or mechanical, including photocopying, recording, or by any information storage and retrieval system with out written permission except in the case of brief quotations embodied in critical articles and reviews. Printed in the United States of America.

Published by The phazelFOZ Company, LLC.
Chicago, Illinois
www.phazelfoz.com

Library of Congress Number on File

ISBN 978-0-9988803-2-7 (Hardcover)

Release your inner nerd.

Dedicated To

Grae, Audrey, Alfie & Elliot

Table of Hilarious Content

Band Nerds Poetry From The 13th Chair   7

The Marching Band Nerds Handbook   157

Band Nerds Confessions & Confusion   287

The Marching Band Nerds Awards   467

Bonus Material   559

BAND NERDS
Poetry From The 13th Chair Trombone Player

By
DJ Corchin

Illustrated by
Dan Dougherty

BAND NERDS
Poetry From The 13th Chair Trombone Player

By DJ Corchin

"DJ must have been a fly on the wall of my band room for the last thirty years! I read, smiled and reflected on people who have all been a part of my band (and my life) over the years. Every once in a while, I found that I was looking in a mirror - and that made me smile, too. As you read these poems, you'll see the face and remember the name of each of these people... You'll remember the great times shared with all of the characters...heck, you may even remember the special smell of a well used band room...then you'll smile, too."

Greg Bimm
Director of Bands; Marion Catholic High School, Chicago Heights, IL

"I'm a band nerd. I admit it. My entire life has been spent playing in, conducting and teaching bands. I am in this book along with my friends, teachers and students. And you know what? DJ is right... they are special people and I like them all. It was a lot of fun to have my life reflected in this book."

Donald DeRoche
Director of Bands; DePaul Univeristy, Chicago, IL

"Coming from a professional 19th chair band geek who is still searching for her "ultimate mouthpiece," I can't think of a better way to cherish the unique inner world of life in the band! These poems prove that participation in school music goes beyond fulfilling an arts credit...it creates a sense of pride, belonging, and humor both on stage and off. Kudos to DJ for creating a hilarious and original work for anyone who has spent even just one day in band class!"

Amy McCabe
Trumpeter/Cornetist;
"The President's Own" United States Marine Band.

"'Band Nerds' is a look inside what must be the band room in every school - and a look back at my own inner band nerd. Even years removed, DJ's spot on humor brings a sheepish smile to my face as I remember those days and all the 'characters' that have been part of MY music history."

Scott McCormick
President and CEO of Music for All, Inc.
and the Bands of America and Orchestra America divisions

"DJ Corchin's book provides a rare, in-depth insight into our nation's band sub-culture, a medium that continues to provide emotional sanctuary for so many of our best and brightest young people. His poetry opens a window for us former band members to reflect fondly upon our school years, while it also garners an opportunity for the rest of the world to understand the powerful force which drives so many of us to success in life."

Dave Morrison
Illinois Teacher of the Year 2003 and Director of Bands (retired);
Prospect High School, Mt Prospect, IL

"What a KICK! You'll find yourself laughing and sometimes crying at the wonderful words DJ Corchin has articulately and artfully put on paper in this collection of poems. Using the power of poetry anyone who is in band, was in band, knows someone in band, or knew someone in band will enjoy this book. Whether humorous or harsh, poignant or pathetic, inspiring or irritating - either way DJ hopes you will choose to 'laugh it off.' Helping the reader to rise above the stereotyping that unfortunately sometimes shapes our perceptions and personalities, this book taps into the healthy therapeutic nature of humor to laugh with - and sometimes at - the wonderfully strange world of **Band Nerds**."

Fran Kick
Educational consultant,
speaker and author who inspires kids to KICK IT IN®

"Being a member of a band family made the high school years bearable! These poems bring back so many memories as they perfectly describe my time in the flute section. (Thank GOD I switched to bassoon!) This would have been THE book to read when skipping English class... hanging out in the band room of course! A must read for band students both young and old."

Camilla M. Stasa
Director of Participant Relations, Music for All (Bands of America)

"This fun, humorous, interesting, journey through life via membership in the band is a delightful read. These poems joggled my memory and took me back to many wonderful friends, places and sounds. Change the names and this is my life. At times we've all stood out, couldn't get it, and/or the entire world was conspiring against us. It's called growing up and these poems capture the entire exciting roller coaster ride, providing you were fortunate enough to find the band room during your childhood. Enjoy, smile, laugh and be thankful, you were in the band!"

Brian Logan
Director of Bands; Wheeling High School, Wheeling, IL

BAND NERDS
Poetry From The 13th Chair Trombone Player

By DJ Corchin

The phazelFOZ Company, LLC

BAND NERDS POETRY FROM THE 13TH CHAIR TROMBONE PLAYER
Copyright © 2009 By DJ Corchin

All rights reserved. No part of this book may be reproduced or transmitted in any form or by any means, electronic or mechanical, including photocopying, recording, or by any information storage and retrieval system without written permission except in the case of brief quotations embodied in critical articles and reviews. Printed in the United States of America.

Published by The phazelFOZ Company, LLC.
Chicago, Illinois
www.phazelfoz.com

Illustrations, book, and jacket design by Dan Dougherty
Edited by Mike Hurley

Library of Congress Number   2009901301

ISBN 978-0-9819645-0-8 (Paperback)

Stereotypes

We all know stereotypes can have a terrible effect. They're harmful to a person's ego, self-worth, and self-esteem. There's nothing more frustrating than being categorized before someone even takes the time to talk with you. Whether it involves race, gender, age, religion, sexuality, or something as small as what activities you're in, stereotypes are unfortunately here to stay. There's not going to be a huge revolution of the human mind that says, "You know what? I don't need to categorize things within 3 seconds of seeing them." So the only weapon we have against stereotypes, in this non-doctor's, non-psychologist's, non-philanthropist's, non-professor's, non-philosopher's opinion, is *choice*. We can choose to let them shape us, or we can choose to write a silly poem book about them and laugh it off.
You choose.

Dedicated to

Dr. Wesley Vos
L.J. Hancock
&
Jonathan "Lance" Harmeling

13th Chair

I was 13th chair in my elementary band.
I was as discouraged as I could be.
The teacher told me it was alphabetized,
But my name starts with C.

And as time went on, I never moved.
Last chair is where I'd sit.
But 7 years later I'm finally first
'Cause everyone else had quit.

Distress Call

Hello 911? Please help me
I don't know what to do!
My band is spinning out of control,
The room's become a zoo.
There's so much going on right now
I'm not sure where to start.
Jenny lit her reeds on fire,
The tuba lit his fart.
The trombones are in the corner
Playing truth or dare.
Which I guess explains
Why John McBain
Is in his underwear.
There's French Horns in the rafters.
Piccolos breaking stands.
Saxes kissing one another,
And baritones eating crayons.

The percussion are hosting a seance,
I'm scared for my life.
Oh God they have a dead goat over there
And a picture of my wife!
The trumpets are in the practice room,
But not to practice early.
They grabbed a freshman by the toes
And proceeded with a swirly.
I've lost control. I'm not in charge.
Come quick it can't be far.
Please they're banging down my office door
With the muffler of my car!

Enough

I didn't really believe it,
'Til I looked in and seen it,
But nevertheless it's true.
Tom's tuba could talk,
It got up and walked,
And said, "the heck with you I'm through."

Ultimate Mouthpiece

Now and forever
My mistakes shall cease,
'Cause I bought myself
An ultimate mouthpiece.
Never again will I miss a note,
Will you hear a gerplat,
A patoot, or a splote.
I place it in my horn,
It's magic you'll see,
'Cause my fingers move
Faster than faster can be.
...did I mention I can now hit a double quadruple G!
Even though I'm only twelve
A hundred grand at least,
Is what I should be paid for me
To play my ultimate mouthpiece.

Euphonium

Nothing rhymes with euphonium.
Except the word plutonium.
So I'll just use euphonium
And finally write this poem.

Revenge

It's ok to gawk and laugh out loud
Making fun of me a bit.

I'll just place my spit valve on your head
Count to three and let'er rip!

New Private Teacher

Wow thank you Mrs. Nevenshire.
You were sent from heaven.
Jimmy plays three times a day
Since you teach all his lessons.

I Have An Itch

I have an itch.
I have an itch.
I can not scratch
Or move an inch.
I'm at attention.
I can not twitch.
Oh what to do.
I have an itch.

Closed Eyes

I'd like to tell you about a friend
I met last year this time.
He was a pretty special kid
You see my friend is blind.

That didn't stop him from playing his horn
He just listened once and knew it.
He'd close his eyes and finger along
I'm not sure how he'd do it.

I asked him why he closed his eyes
His answer quite profound.
He said, "People tend to stare at them,
Not focus on my sound."

I thought, how true the world we have
We look before we listen.
Maybe if we closed our eyes
The world would pay attention.

From Me To You

Musical. Instrument. Digital. Interface.
Think it up. Plug it in. Send it off to cyberspace.
Post it up. Send it out. Surf around. Find the link.
Grab the tune. Plug it in. Start it up and data sync.

I Seem To Have A Problem 1

I seem to have a problem.
I'm not sure where to start.
Every time I play my oboe
I also play a fart.

The Great Kiss Off of '96

The great kiss off contest of '96
Was the best that's ever been.
Pride was at stake for the hearts of the band
To quit was a mortal sin.

Faces were red, cheeks were blown,
Eyes popped out of their sockets.
But nothing compared to Jared DuCaine
And the trick he pulled out of his pocket.

He stepped to the crowd all smiley and proud
And took out his special mouthpiece.
Unbelievably small it measured around
The size of a straw at least.

Jared put it to his face, buckled down hard,
Took a big breath and blew.
A screeching E flat was the note that he picked
And boy it came barreling through.

At first he was normal, even cool and calm,
But then he began to change.
His eyes started to water, his knees shook,
You could tell that he was in pain.

But that didn't stop Big Jared - no way
As the sweat dripped down from his nose.
Bulges began to pop from his head
And air shot out of his toes.

He started leaking fluids
From every place and more-so.
His left eye shot out, he blew a vein,
A rib popped out of his torso.

But Jared kept playing even louder
Until he finally just gave out.
He ripped the sucker off his face
And took off half his mouth.

The crowd erupted and rose to their feet,
As the hero picked up his lips.
His feat would be called an historic event.
The Great Kiss Off Of '96.

Guard Captain

This girl said she was guard captain.
I had reason not to believe her.
She claimed to be able to throw a twelve
So I said I'd like to see her.
With a bend of the knee and a twist of the wrist,
The saber cut through the air.
She ran in fear
As it sliced her ear
A sight I could not bear.

I Got Your Pass Right Here!

I'm sorry I'm late to math class,
But it really wasn't my fault.
Our director made us march ahead
And refused to give a halt.
We must have gone six miles,
Through mud and sleet and snow.
We jumped a fence and swam a creek,
Climbed mountains high and low.
He made us march past Jimmy's house.
You know, the one with the rabid dog?
It chased us for at least eight blocks.
We lost it in the fog.
By the time we made it back to school,
There were broken bones and shattered glass.
The nurse amputated my left toe,
So do you really need a pass?

Saxes In Concert Band

Play Softer! Play Softer!
That's all they ever say.
They tell me to play piano,
But it's written forte.

And when I raise my hand
To tell them what's there,
They say, "you're saxes in concert band,
I really don't care."

The Triangle Player From Del Torre

I am the triangle player from Del Torre.
Everybody knows my story.
With a ting and a ping
I make women sing,
'Cause I am the triangle player from Del Torre.

Operation

Mom, oh Mom, can I please get
That special operation?
The one that allows you to play the trombone
As a full time occupation.

What do you mean you don't understand?
Where do you think the slide goes?
It goes down your throat
and out your rear
My brother told me so.

Drummer

Flam tap, Flam tap, Flam tap, Splot!
Flam Accent, Flam Accent, Shot!
I can drum in perfect beat.
Paradittle, paradittle, kiss my feet.

Rough, Rough, Rough, Flog
Now you're sounding like a dog.
Herta, Herta, Herta, smack.
I'll put a drum stick in your crack.

Scale Test

Why do we have to learn the hard ones?
We never see more than 4 flats.
That's like telling us we're gonna use
All the lessons learned in math.

And we only ever see a sharp
If we're orchestra volunteers.
Why should we be penalized
For helping out our peers?

The key of B is meaningless,
To me it's just plain wrong.
How about I stick with C
And we can move along.

Drum MAJOR Crush

I love it when she yells at me.
I lose it when she looks at me.
She tells me what to do you see
And puts me in my spot.

Turn right, flank left, toes off the ground.
I love she bosses me around.
The stricter that she gets I've found
The more I think she's hot.

My Uniform

I got it! I got it!
I got it today!
My uniform is here.
Hoorah! Hooray!

So what it's too big.
So what it's too small.
So what that it smells
And don't fit at all.

It's mine, I'm happy.
It's mine I say.
My uniform is here.
Hoorah! Hooray!

Secret Weapon

An army recruiter came by yesterday
I'm really not sure why.
He watched us spin our rifles 'round
Then pointed to the sky.

He wanted us to join his ranks.
Airborne unit he said.
I had to tell him the guns weren't real
And this was all pretend.

But he didn't care 'bout the guns in the air
So I started to hold my breath.
He said, "We'll drop you in, forget your spins,
Just talk them all to death."

True Friends

I'm not sure why we did it.
But we did it nonetheless.
We locked our friend up in the john,
Shut the lights and left.

He happened to play tuba,
So it was clear that he was missing.
We continued to play our warm-up scales
While he was reminiscing.

The teacher asked us where he was.
We shook our heads about.
We hadn't decided either way,
If we would let him out.

Skip

I met a tuba player named Skip.
I tried to giv'm a tip.
No matter how hard he tried,
He sat there and sighed,
'Cause he only had one lip.

Inspiration

First of all, congrats to you
For making it all this way.
We've come so far if you recall
And remember our first day.

And now we're here at concert time.
So exciting from the start.
Just remember all you've learned
And make the music from your heart.

I know you expect a story or two
To inspire you for luck.
I'm not quite sure what's left to say,
But whatever you do, don't suck.

I Seem To Have A Problem 2

I seem to have a problem
I'm not sure why it is.
Once I put my uniform on
I have to take a whiz.

First Chair

I am the first chair.
A very important role.
Everyone looks up to me.
At least that's what I'm told.

I have special duties
Passing music to the rest.
I am the first chair I say
Of all the 3rd part clarinets.

Challenge

I challenge you, you stupid fool
Tomorrow right at noon.
You'll lose your chair and I'll sit there
Before I'm through with you.

> I challenge YOU, you petty turd.
> Yes that's right, I said it.
> You suck, by luck you got real close
> And now you're gonna get it.

Oh please you tool, I'll walk right in
And put you right to tears.
Mentally you'll be a wreck.
Need therapy for years.

> You challenge me? Are you insane?
> I can't imagine why.
> I'll smack your sister in her face
> And make your mother cry!

The Opener

I think you should play percussion.
I'm not sure flute is for you.
Not trumpet, horn, or saxophone.
None of these will do.

How can I put this nicely?
How can I say this right?
Um, you could open a can of soup
With your massive overbite.

Juggernaut

Westmoore High School won again
But it's really no surprise.
They've never ever ever lost.
In this I tell no lies.

Their director served the army.
Their guard captain on Broadway.
Between the two, they tend to spend
More cash than Uruguay.

Their drums are made of solid gold.
Flags tailored by Versace.
Their meals prepared and catered by
The famous chef Lagasse.

They rent the entire Astrodome
For a Wednesday night rehearsal.
Their performances filmed and marketed by
The staff at Universal.

There's no secret why they won.
No one stood a chance.
They could afford a jet to fly
The judges all to France.

Magic Oboe

Yesterday I sat down and played
What I thought was a normal B flat.
But when I made a sound
I looked to the ground.
Scott Miller morphed into a rat!

I thought, "this is cool, the power I have,"
And proceeded to have some fun.
I played a low G
And that jerk Tom McGee
Was suddenly dressed as a nun.

I couldn't resist and had to persist
To give all the tubas green hair.
The saxes were dead
The flutes had no legs
And suddenly I was first chair!

I play a magic oboe.
Don't laugh, you know what I'll do?
I'll tap on the keys
And blow on the reeds
So your mouthpiece tastes like poo!

I Suck

Oh man not again, I cracked a note
And my valve? Yep, it stuck.
I can't tongue for spit
I must admit.
Jeez, I really suck.

Secret Room

Deep behind the band room
There's a room we like to store
Our instruments and costume racks
But that's not what it's for.

Only students enter in.
Teachers do not dare.
We call it the secret make out room
Guess what we do there?

Stuck

My saber's stuck in a star up high
It's lost somewhere up in the sky.
If you see it sticking out,
Please tell me of it's whereabouts.

Jazzer

I don't play that kind
Of music I find
It's just not appealing to me.

I don't march in line
Play 8th notes in time
Jazz is my gig, you see.

Mr. Smith

Beware of Mr. Smith
Director of the band.
He can make you poop your pants,
With a single stroke of his hand.
He's fat, he's bald, he has fake teeth,
At least that I can tell.
The yellow sweat stains under his arms
Have finally begun to smell.
Once in a while he'll give you a smile
But anyone will tell ya,
You can't trust him because that grin
Means he's gonna fail ya.

Band Dads

What do you need, what can I move?
Is there something I can getch'ya?
No one moves faster than me and my crew,
If you do it's 'cause we letch'ya.
We've hauled percussion through sleet and snow,
Through hail and acid rain.
There's no job too heavy or task too hard
For we do not feel pain.
Dedication runs through our veins
For our children's musical lives.
The more time we spend catering to them,
The less we do with our wives!

F and B Flat

Will everyone please play
An F and B flat?
That's all that I want.
An F and B flat.
You don't need to laugh
At something like that.
Will someone please play
AN F'n B FLAT!?

Awkwardly Band

I recently joined the awkwardly band,
That's led by an equally awkwardly man.
It has a unique and awkwardly sound.
It's where the weird people are awkwardly found.

One boy plays an awkward recorder
And seems to have an awkward disorder.
No wonder he's in the awkwardly band.
He seems to play with three awkwardly hands.

And there's the girl who's awkwardly shy.
We think it's because of her awkwardly eyes.
It's not that they're black or awkwardly red.
But they're on the wrong side of her awkwardly head.

It's awkwardly awkward to play in this place,
With it's awkwardly style and awkwardly taste.
Awkwardly led by that awkwardly man,
I recently joined the awkwardly band.

On Fire

"Jimmy why are you moving?
The whole band's at a halt."

                        "I'm sorry sir, but I have to say,
                          It's really not my fault."

"Oh no, who else is running around
As if they were on fire?"

                        "That's the point I'm trying to make,
                          The situation's kind of dire."

I Seem To Have A Problem 3

I seem to have a problem.
I'm not sure what to git.
If I play the clarinet
I suck up my own spit?!

The Letter

Dear Mom,
    I'm writing to you today because
    I have a tiff with how you raised me.
    I don't understand, I do all I can
    And no one seems to praise me.
    I play high notes, the kind that screech,
    My scales at two-twenty-two.
    I play my trumpet perfectly
    So the problem must be with you.
    Please don't be mad or even sad,
    I'm being honest like you taught me.
    Just admit how bad you screwed up
    And I'll put this all behind me.

(The Reply)

Dear Son,
    You're dumb, you stupid fool,
    Idiotic I'd say at best.
    Don't blame me because they see
    You're more obnoxious than the rest.
    You wouldn't listen all those years.
    Just blew louder in my face.
    I'm glad that all the pretty girls
    Put your sorry butt in place.
    And as long as we're being honest
    There's something that should be said.
    Don't talk to me again like that.
    I know you wet your bed.

Hmm...

She's looking at me
'Cross the band once again.
Is she smiling or squeezing out
That note at measure 10?

French Horns are so confusing.
Are they happy or are they mad?
They always seem to make a face
Both joyful and somewhat sad.

If she could just tell me
What she's thinking either way.
I'll know to either run like hell,
Or ask her out today.

Hope

I wanna tell you something.
I'm not sure if I should.
Something I'm not proud of.
Something that's not good.

I think I've fallen really hard
For someone not in band.
I know I'm not supposed to but,
She's gorgeous, tall, and tan.

I see her after school sometimes
Hanging with her guy.
I hope one day I'll live to say
I actually said hi.

I Seem To Have A Problem 4

I seem to have a problem.
I'm not sure who to tell.
Every time I play the trumpet
My ego hurts like hell.

Busting Out

I didn't want to say it
But your uniform's too small.
Your bosom's really busting out
And we can see it all.

A Truly Weird Audition

I want center snare
Not because of my flare
Or due to my natural wit.

I truly believe
That I can achieve
Perfection while down in the splits.

Toes Up

I never thought I'd see the day
Someone's toes too high.
But Alex's feet were straight up and down,
I couldn't believe my eyes.

The Pit Crew From Calmanti

Our pit crew from Calmanti
Is known throughout the land,
We're able to move in 10 seconds flat
And build apartments for the band.
We have only the best parents
Recruited for this routine,
With physical training and strategy plans
We're a well oiled machine.

Mr. Jones the nuclear physicist.
He builds our jet powered carts.
Mr. Sindle runs the mafia,
So he steals all our parts.
Mr. Briar works at NASA,
For satellite communications.
Mrs. Niles is a supreme court judge
And handles accusations.

Mr. Grell works at the Pentagon
To get our fake I.D.s.
Mrs. Landy's in the CIA
For operations over-seas.
Mikey Keller's cousin
Flies Stealths and F-16s.
Mr. Trent is in command
Of a Navy Submarine.

The Pit Crew from Calmanti
Is a legend near and far.
Our tales are often midnight dreams,
And stories told at bars.

There's no job we can not handle.
No country we can not run.
But if all you need is percussion moved
Consider it already done.

Journey

We went to contest the other day
And the judges said we stunk.
But I would have to disagree
That what we did was junk.

We spent 3 months just practicing
For the pieces we would play.
We felt ourselves improve a bit
Each and every day.

When we started out this year
No one played a scale.
Now we play all twelve of them
Before the Bach Chorales.

It doesn't matter what they say
With their ridicule and scorn.
The judges don't mean squat to us
'Cause we finally play our horns.

Women.

I had to break it off with Jill.
It really wouldn't work.
It's not my fault I made top band.
But apparently I'm the jerk.

She said if I really loved her
I wouldn't have done so good.
We'd both be in the low band,
Like the way a couple should.

Well, I told her she was crazy.
Farewell, goodbye, so long.
It's not my fault she sucked at flute,
But apparently I was wrong.

Hot Cross Buns

Hot...Cross...Buns.
Hot...Cross...Buns.
I can not believe I'm doing
This...is...dumb.

I Seem To Have A Problem 5

I seem to have a problem.
I'm not sure what to do.
I want to play percussion
But have no attitude.

Old Fashioned

No girl will be in my snare line.
Not while I'm alive.
That doesn't seem to work for me.
With her I can not thrive.
She'll screw up all the chemistry.
It's always been us dudes.
Plus, the harness couldn't possibly fit
Over her gigantic boo...um...hair.
It's not that I'm against all girls
Or hate women you see.
It's that most of them in our band
Well, they just play better than me!

John McDoogal

There's John McDoogal
Who plays on his flugel,
The sweet sweet sounds of the blues.

He'll play there all night
For the women in sight.
There's no way he could possibly lose.

But the jokes played on him
As the women all grin
And wink at John in surprise.

The ladies all laughed
As he let out a gasp
And noticed his wide open fly.

Carpenters

Double reeds walk the line.
This we've always known.
They don't buy their reeds, the heck with that,
They go and make their own.

They chisel away for hours on end,
Skilled with chunks of wood.
I'd hire them to build my house.
I really think they could.

Microphone

Mr. Harris swallowed his microphone
And he just can't get it free.
So we hear him almost all the time.
Like when he has to pee.

We've heard him with the principal.
We've heard him passing gas.
We've heard him singing stupid songs
And kissing Mrs. Nash!

2nd Chair Princess

Now you listen here
Mr. Band Director man.
I should be first chair
Not that horse with a tan.
Are you nuts? Are you blind?
Are you feeling ok?
There's no way she beat me.
You're wrong all the way.
She's stupid, she's ugly,
She's the world's biggest nerd.
She's the joke of the town.
Have you not heard?
I'm so much better.
You can't even compare.
Her fashion is terrible
Not to mention her hair.
So I can't play my scales
And can't match a tone.
It won't mean a thing
When I get my mom on the phone.

Pride

I am the trumpet player.
I can play high.
I am the trumpet player,
With a gleam in my eye.
I can play loud.
I can play tough.
I love to play fast.
I can't get enough.
There's no part too hard,
Too tricky, too sly.
No one plays better than me.
I'd rather die.
I am the trumpet player.
I am the best.
Don't step to me 'cause
I'll turn your sorry butt inside out,
Kick you in your face and make sure you cry
so long your mamma is embarrassed to call you her child.

Joe

Joe talks too much about our band.
We think that he's obsessed.
Joe doesn't really date that much.
I'm sure you could've guessed.

Salute

Excuse me nurse do you have some ice?
I'm sorry I'm starting to cry.
It seems that when I saluted the crowd,
I hit myself right in the eye.

Saxamaphone

Saxamaphone, Saxamaphone,
I play the saxamaphone.
It sounds really neat
'Cause I have no teeth
When I play my saxamaphone.

School Horn

I brought home my new school horn today.
I opened it up almost right away.
My gosh that funk!
It stinks like skunk!
I brought back my new school horn today.

The Ghost of That's Freshman Pete

There's a legend that goes back about 80 years.
Before there's computers and mp3 gear.
A freshman joined band and on his first week,
He became known as That's Freshman Pete.

Horns would go up, his would go down.
They would go left, and he'd turn around.
The whole band would march
And come to a turn,
But Pete would keep going
Not even concerned.
He marched to his own
Awkwardly beat.
But they would just shrug
'Cause That's Freshman Pete.

Until one day, they came to a curve.
Pete kept on going, it was really absurd.
Normally he would stop and return,
But this time was different, real cause for concern.

Sooner than later he marched from their sight.
He didn't come back all day or all night.
In fact he didn't come back ever again,
And nobody knew what happened to him.

It's been said that since that day,
He still haunts this school today.
His ghost still marches in the streets,
Don't be scared, That's Freshman Pete.

Mistake

Did you hear that?
He cracked the G sharp.
I mean he's a pro
and <u>still</u> missed his part.

I don't care if he's nice,
I don't care if he's good.
I paid forty bucks,
So he'll play like he should.

No I won't settle down,
This isn't a joke.
He's getting paid
And I'm really broke!

True Player

All the ladies want to date me.
It's because I play trombone.
Ever since I switched from sax
They just won't leave me alone.

Torture

I love to mess with Greg Tulaine
Who lives with perfect pitch.
I'll dip my lips a quarter tone
Just to watch him twitch.

I know it bugs him really bad,
So of course I push it more.
Once I hit a half a step he
Starts convulsing on the floor.

Yes it seems a little cruel,
But it's something he deserves.
He always says I'm out of tune,
Can you believe his nerve?

Useless Talent

Have you seen the dancing euphonium player
Who plays for Blayton Prep?
They say he's able to do 4 turns
And not fall out of step.

He leaps, he twirls, he pops and locks
With toes that touch the clouds.
He'll play a heart felt melody
And "robot" for the crowds.

It's pretty darn amazing
What this guy can do.
But there's no jobs for dancing euphonium players
I know of none, do you?

Bad Day

My day is going really bad
I'm not sure why that is.
I failed my test with a 42
And fought with my friend Liz.

I tripped while walking to P.E.
And everyone just laughed.
I couldn't remember my locker's code
So I kicked it 'till it cracked.

My boyfriend dumped me during lunch
He did it in a note.
We had to do a fire drill
And someone stole my coat.

I walked into the bathroom,
But the stalls there had no doors.
It didn't take me long to see
The urinals weren't decor.

I find it's really hard to smile
I'm not sure how I can.
But things are looking better now
'Cause I'm on my way to band.

Audition

It was once said
That lying in bed
A little girl went nuts.
'Cause she stayed up all night
And trembled in fright
Her audition turned out a bust.

How A Trumpet Plays A Duet

Let's play a duet.
Let's play it today.
I'll play the high part
And you go away.

Disturbing

I think of band all the time,
I think of it in the shower.
I think of it while I'm rehearsing a play
Or outside picking flowers.

I think of band while playing catch
And almost all I do.
But what's really weird is I think of band
While making out with you!

Natural High

I love the sound of low notes
On my flute that I just bought.
They sound so rich and lovely.
Just like I was taught.

I've become renowned for them.
The low note player in town.
I would play them all the time,
But I get dizzy, then fall down.

Medieval Marching

This year's show was a medieval theme
And quite a sight to bear.
Every detail true in fact
And no expense was spared.

We played the extra long trumpets.
Like ones way back in the day.
They didn't have a single valve
One key is all we played.

Somehow we got 3 horses.
Which was very cool at first.
But then we stepped in something brown.
We're sure it wasn't dirt.

The costumes were made of sheep skin.
The jousting was done for real.
The swords landed just one cut.
It was really no big deal.

Then the staff went way too far.
It was a little bit upsetting.
They said for extra G.E. points
We should stage a real beheading!

Juggle

I like to juggle mouthpieces.
I can juggle up to four.
One hit me in the head today.
I don't juggle anymore.

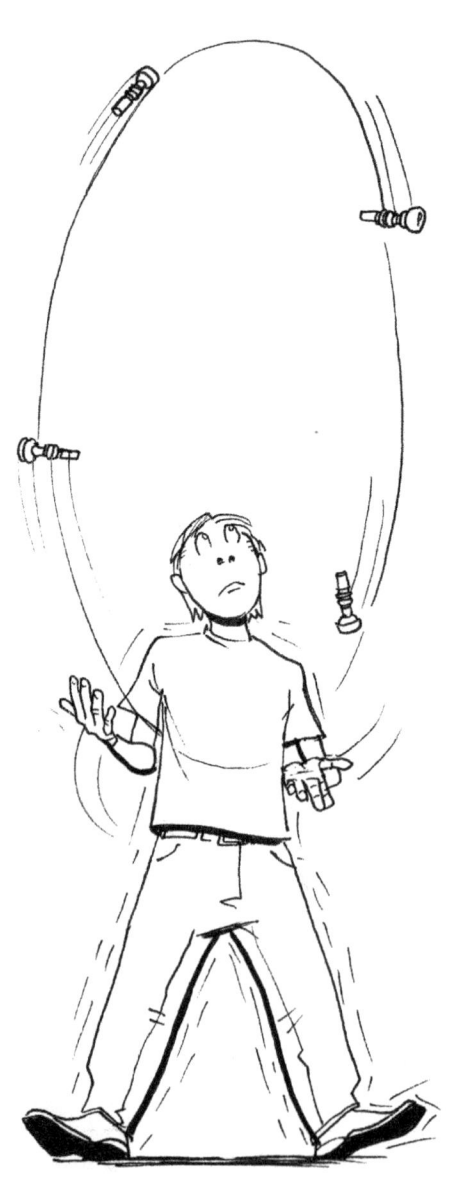

Potential

Yesterday some would say
I received the kiss of death.
Mr. Logan gave the "potential speech"
To me and Jessica Beth.

He said I had "potential."
Whatever the heck that means.
All's I know he didn't pick me
To drive our marching machine.

But he wouldn't let me quit.
I'm not sure how he did it.
He somehow made me change my mind
I simply must admit it.

He told me that I need the band
As much as it needs me.
He was right I must confess
My potential he did see.

Mellophone, Mellophone

Mellophone, Mellophone,
Why do you smellophone?
You can't play in tuneophone.
Too gross to touch.

Mellophone, Mellophone,
What is your dealophone?
Valves are all stuckophone.
I hate you so much.

Balance and Blend

Balance and Blend,
Balance and Blend,
That is the key
To music my friend.

Poor April

What the heck is that?
A duck or crying goose?
No, it must be April Smith,
I guess her reed is loose.

Love-Hate Relationship

What are they doing
Those people back there?
I don't understand them,
They're crazy I swear.
They're loud, they smell,
There's no trace of tact.
They just wiped a booger
All over my back.
They sit there during rehearsal
And count their dumb rests.
The buttheads won't take
Their eyes off my chest.
They drool, they sweat.
A bath? What's that?
They bang on their drums
And poisoned my cat.

They lose all their sticks
Spill pop on the floor.
My gosh, what is that?
A dead rat on the door?
They give out free wedgies
And spit just for laughs.
Tommy the snare drum
Has really bad gas.
They rant and they rave
Hurt people for money.
Most of them think
Diarhhea is funny.
They give me the willies
I just want to puke.
Actually, now that I think about it...
                        they are kinda cute.

Feet

I have unbelievably large feet
So it's easy to march to the beat.
It takes me less time,
To reach my yard line,
But it's hard to be discreet.

Clarinet Jack

Clarinet Jack is what he likes to be called,
With a reed in his mouth when walking the halls.
It's so he can feel that he's always prepared
When Clarinet Jack is needed.

He walks with a cool, confident strut.
And jeans wrap around his cool, confident butt.
He won't let you down no matter the cost
Our expectations are always exceeded.

Confidence

I'm sick and tired of getting punched
Because you don't understand.
You jocks just walk all over me
Because I play in band.
But no longer will you point and gawk,
I've had it up to here.
I don't think you heard me son,
Or else you'd run in fear.
I'm tough, I'm strong, been working out,
I've clearly found my niche.
I'd go so far as to say
I think your mom's a witch.
No no, stay there, no need to swear
Or charge at me like that.
I'll intimidate you with my built-up pecs
…or at least my brand new bat!

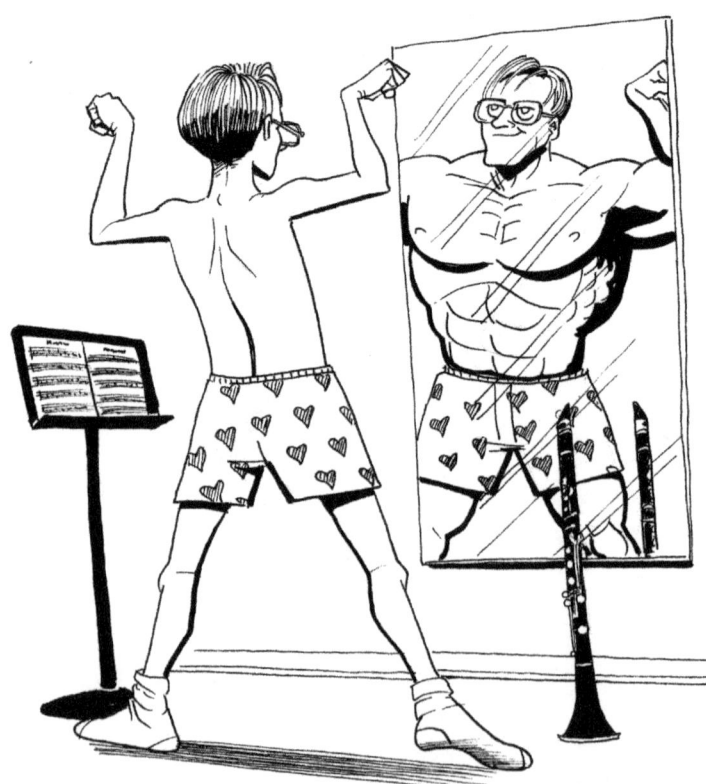

From Bad Audition To Worse

Mom, I know I didn't make the band.
At least with scores you see.
I heard the others play their parts.
They sounded better than me.

But mysteriously I made the cut.
I'm currently first chair.
You put on extra makeup.
Spent an hour on your hair.

I know you want the best for me
And I know I let you down.
Forgive me but I have to ask,
DID YOU HIT ON MR. BROWN?!

Advice

Um, you might want to get off the ground.
It's not where you want to sit.
I know you're not familiar with band,
But that's where we drain our spit.

Annoying

I think I'm finally gonna crack'm
If he doesn't stop his tap'n.
Jam my reed
Into his knee,
Kick him then I'll slap'm.

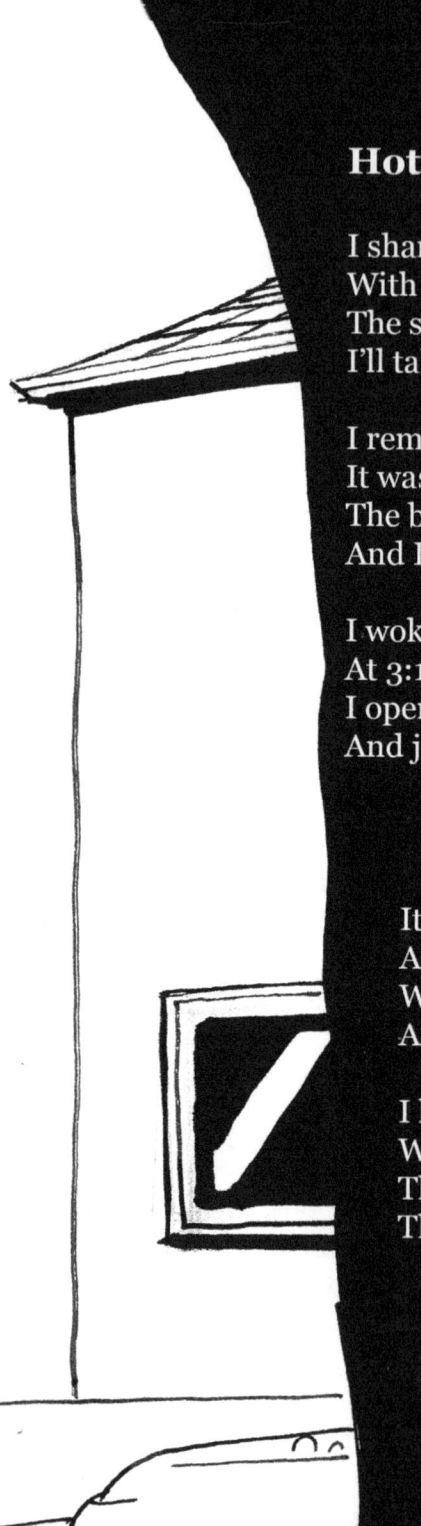

Hot Tub

I shared an awkward moment
With my high school band director.
The story's true I swear to God.
I'll take a lie detector.

I remember it quite clearly.
It was during freshman trip.
The band had gone to some place warm
And I played in the pit.

I woke up hearing talking
At 3:15 a.m.
I opened up my hotel door
And joined the gather'n.

It was me and him plus Tom McLil
And Joe I think was there.
We looked out at the hot tub pool
And we began to stare.

I have to say it shocked us all
What we saw in that tub.
The birds and bees were out that night
The moon shined high above.

He looked at us, we looked at him.
Not knowing what to say.
We bonded for the first time.
Those strangers made our day.

So we closed our doors, went back to bed
And never brought it up.
But we all remember "hot tub" night
As the night we all grew up.

Rookie Band Trip

Something's different about Mr. Sprant.
He just hasn't been the same.
He's been a little "off the beat,"
Since our trip to Spain.
Something about him is peculiar and odd.
Things are just not right.
His hands are shaking, his neck is aching
He claims he's losing his sight.
He blacks out on occasion,
Increased medication,
And sometimes tends to drool.
He used to have hair,
But now he is bare,
Oh how two weeks can be so cruel.

The New Drum Major

Get your toes up!
Get'm up high!
I wanna see the gum on your shoes
And your chin at the sky!
Get those shoulders back buddy,
And suck in that gut.
Put the cheeseburger down
And don't be a klutz.
What's wrong with you kid
That you can't do a flank?
Not heard of deodorant?
You smell kinda rank.
Your technique is all wrong
You're playing is poo,
You look like my dad's butt
Which has zits just like you.
Get yourself at attention.
I didn't say at ease.
Wait Mom, I'm not done yet,
Don't go, I'm just practicing. Come on, Please?

The Ringer

Our lead Alto's Grant Van Singer.
The famous, handsome, jazz soloist ringer.
His notes are so quick,
His licks are so sick,
You won't even notice his four extra fingers.

Too Cool

We read this tune in Jazz band.
It had an amazing groove.
It was so laid back, we couldn't play
So we sat and didn't move.

The whole rehearsal seemed to pass
But it didn't really matter.
The point is that we're being cool
And we'll be called a "jazzer."

I Seem To Have A Problem 6

I seem to have a problem.
I really have to say.
My slide got bent to 90 degrees
Which makes it hard to play.

Tough Love

I love my flute
I love it this much!
I hug it every day
And treat it as such.

I bring it to the store,
To the park, to the zoo.
Why it won't play,
I don't have a clue.

My First Parade

Oh my gosh I'm out of step.
My posture's bad as bad can get.
My toes aren't up, my knees are stiff,
I can not feel my upper lip.
I can't remember all my parts.
I have no clue of where to start.
I think my bibbers lost a clip,
My drawers are out and I might trip.

Lost

I'm no longer a freshman
But still have some questions
And still need some help on my parts.

And I'm not quite a junior
If you don't help me soon you're
Liable to see me depart.

Not sure where I fit in
This band that I sit in
Someone just tell me my place.

A sophomore this season I
Don't see the reason why
Seniors are still in my face.

Just Try It

Go ahead and try it.
Just try it for a week.
Grab a horn and join the band,
Release your inner geek.

Live the life that we live.
Practice night and day.
You just might find you're getting good,
And maybe want to stay.

Famous Last Words

It's not me, honestly.
It's the reed you see
Making me squawk and squeak.
I practiced really hard I swear.
Like 17 minutes last week.

Band Camp

I've heard all the jokes.
I've heard all the lines.
But it doesn't make me frown.

I go to band camp
Once a year,
'Cause man can we get down!

Best Friend

My tuba and me are best of friends,
But not because we talk.
We don't go to movies, braid our hair,
Or take a friendly walk.

It's been good to me ever since,
My mother went to buy it.
It plays in tune, it shines itself.
I even fit inside it.

So when I'm feeling really down,
And need a place to stay.
I crawl inside my tuba bell,
And hang out for the day.

Crazy Drill

This drill is completely crazy.
Dangerous to say the least.
It's got tubas rolling over snares,
And trumpets doing leaps.

The pit is marching on the field.
The guard up in the stands.
The saxes on the field goal posts.
The flutes ride in a van.

There seems to be a bassoon out there.
Ooo...that had to hurt.
Someone call a doctor quick
Or at least a certified nurse.

There's at least three pass thrus, which isn't bad,
Except they're every beat.
I can't read English quite as fast
As I have to move my feet.

I guess it's worth it in the end,
When the audience feels inspired.
But I'm still not sure we need to have
A burning ring of fire!

Choosing Time

The trumpet is too loud.
The flute is too high.
The violin's too screechy,
And the drums make me cry.

The tuba's too fat.
The oboe is sick.
I can't bear to hear
A licorice stick.

The piano's too plain.
The sax is too gold.
The bassoon is too weird looking
And too hard to hold.

The baritone's too boring
And reeks a foul stench.
The french horn is so stupid
I'M NOT EVEN FRENCH!

I wanna play an instrument.
I'm not sure which one.
There are so many to choose from
But most are just dumb.

The cello's too big
And I hate to sing.
Did I mention that music's
My favorite thing?

Podium

Mr. Block's podium
Is five and a half feet tall.
He says it's so we can see him well,
But I don't think that's all.

I think there's something up there.
Something we don't know.
We seem to hear strange noises
While he conducts us with his toes.

I Seem To Have A Problem 7

I seem to have a problem.
I'm not sure where to go.
I always play way out of tune.
My teacher told me so.

Skat

Do ba do dot
BaSquee ba do zot
Ba ratata boom, sha boom.

Veetle do dam,
Sha eetle rum sham
Ba Fatata shoom, ba oom.

Secret Envy

Being the low brass type
I just don't admit,
Thinking of woodwinds.
I'd have to quit.

But there's one thing
I wish I could have.
The fingerless gloves
Just…feel…so…"bad."

The New 4th Trumpet

"Sally, what is Jimmy doing here
   With that guilty little smear
      Which makes my bloodstream boil?"

"Well he got switched from third
   After they heard
      He likes to drink valve oil."

The Plea

I don't want to switch to bassoon,
I like playing the flute.
I won't play that ugly thing,
Not me, I'm way too cute.

I mean there's like a hundred pieces!
That's way too many parts.
I wouldn't know just what to do.
I'm really not that smart.

What the heck's a bocal?
Some green growth on your toe?
The buttons are too spread out,
And I refuse to play that low.

My parents smoke like crazy,
That wouldn't be so good.
'Cause the only instruments we have
Are all made from wood.

So please don't make me switch.
I'm really not your choice.
You better stop harassing me
Or I'll have to switch to voice.

Pop Stars

What if pop stars were in band?
What instruments would they play?
How would they be looked at?
Would they be as cool today?

What if life was different?
Like the other way around.
What if band nerds that we've grown to love
Became the stars in town?

Tossing

I spent last week, ALL last week,
Learning to toss my flag.
I threw it up
And now I'm stuck.
My catching's really bad.

Star Quarterback

I'm just a simple quarterback
Who likes to play in the band.
I don't understand why that makes me
Any less of a man.

Score Order

Who made up this order?
I don't understand.
All the small instruments on top,
Of a very big band.

Why are they more important
Then the rest of us here
That they're first on the list,
And the first to appear.

It's not fair I say,
No not fair at all.
This score order thing
Is really just wrong.

They've gone to a new level.
They're really quite unkind.
They say because of the score order,
That they're first in line.

They're first to get a drink,
On the bus, in the door.
They won't give me the time of day,
To say hi is a chore.

It's not fair I say,
No not fair one bit.
That I have to regret
The instrument I picked.

Tuba Dinner

Thanks for coming over here
I'm starving to say the least.
You'll want to get some extra help,
Us tubas like to feast.

For starters I'll take a metric ton
Of chips and spicy sauce.
No I'm not kidding I said a ton
Don't make me get your boss.

For the next three courses bring some rolls
7 white, 5 Rye, 2 Kaiser.
Also bring a truck of chili.
Now for the appetizers.

I'll have a steak, the biggest you got
No actually bring me two.
For sides I'll have a cheeseburger rare
And four pounds of ribs will do.

This all sounds good but not enough
Do you have something filling?
Like a hippo or a humpback whale,
Something definitely worth grilling.

For dessert I'll take it easy.
Like some chocolate flavored moose.
Not the kind in a glass, the kind that eats grass.
Geez you have no use.

There's nothing I enjoy much more
Than a snack to end my day.
Please wrap up all the extra grease
Or I'll refuse to pay.

Soli Solo

Soli Solo I'm next in line.
Soli Solo it is a crime.
Soli Solo we play our scales.
Soli Solo I just might fail.

The Boners

Let me introduce you
To a group of my friends.
They make up their names
And like to pretend
That they're some sort of hero
You think they've outgrown
This childish obsession
About their trombones.

There's Zeus and Juice
And Big Daddy Fly.
Who always just brags
'Bout the size of his "slide."

It never impressed
Lady Laura one bit,
But she did tend to smile
At Booger and Zit.
Of course Dookie and Bird
Just laughed all the time.
And Tinny Fitzgerald,
Well he's into crime.

It's an unusal gang
Of an abnormal brand.
But with no Boners around
The band would be bland.

Sabor Latino

My favorite type of musical style
Is Latin because it moves us.
El Ritmo gets me go'n
Sacudo mis caderas.

Me gusta tocar la trompeta,
And the spanish guitar is sweet.
The style moves mi corazón.
It's a flavor that can't be beat.

O.C.D.

I gotta oil my valves
I gotta gett'm slick.
I have to do it everyday
Or else they're gonna stick.

I scrub them up and down.
I polish day and night.
My instrument is super clean
I finally got it right.

Last Show Of The Year

It's way too cold out here.
Way too cold by far.
My breath I see a mile away.
My snot is forming bars.

My ears are burning, my knees are locked,
It's difficult to swing.
It's hard to do a jazz show,
When these gloves don't mean a thing :)

I have to do my solo,
But I'm feeling kinda dumb.
I'm not quite sure what note I'm on,
My lips are totally numb!

Feeling It

Oboes move around too much
When they play with pure emotion.
They say it's 'cause they're "feeling it"
But to me it's just commotion.

Family

I know we moan and gripe about
How we treat each other.
But the truth is that I really care,
I love you like my brothers.

And whenever things at home get rough
The band room's where I'll be,
To share my life with all of you,
My one true family.

Band Nerds

We're doctors and lawyers
Who did well in school.
We're entrepeneurs
Who own their own pools.

We're accountants, and surgeons
And chem engineers.
We're pitchers and catchers
Who've conquered their fears.

We're colonels and pilots
And designers of trucks.
We're software programmers
With two million bucks.

Music's among us,
Wherever you look,
There's band nerds around us
Even reading this book.

Peace with a whole lotta hair grease.

See ya.

A Very Sincere Band Nerd Thank You To:

Mom
Scott
Jessica
Brian Logan
Mike Hurley
Diane Rawlinson
Jason Wick
Louis Kholodovsky
Donald DeRoche
Camilla Stasa
Fran Kick
Scott McCormick
Amy McCabe
Mike Madonia
Dave Morrison
Dan Dougherty
Mike Pickard
Greg Bimm
Meredith Gaffke

To everyone who's shown up for me...I Love You.

The Marching
BAND NERDS
Handbook
*Rules from **The 13th Chair** Trombone Player*

By
DJ Corchin

Illustrated By **Dan Dougherty**

Dedicated to

T.S.

*From the outside looking in, no one understands it.
From the inside looking out, no one can explain it.*

"Joining us"... from The 13th Chair Trombone Player, a fun and insightful look at the crazy world of Marching Band! DJ Corchin has done it again. Through his "rules" DJ, takes the activity we love and shows us measure by measure why we love it. I declare The Marching Band Nerds Handbook to be required reading for all incoming band Freshman. (Also Seniors, Parents, Directors, Administrators and... well, you get where I'm going here...) Go for it... Break Ranks!"

Chuck Henson
The "Voice" of Bands of America

"DJ has done it again! He has mixed wit and wisdom into a trek through band memories. If you have been a part of a marching band family, you will have faces from your past to match these pages. If you have not been a part of marching band yet, you may see a bit of the future. Enjoy and laugh. Remember. (Or prepare!) Be sure to take the time to see the many valuable lessons, too."

Greg Bimm
Director of Bands
Marian Catholic High School, Chicago Heights, IL

"DJ Corchin is good medicine. His ability to examine the marching world from a slightly different angle delivers a healthy dose of equal parts humor and inspiration. The Marching Band Nerds Handbook is a perfect prescription that is sure to keep band students, directors, and parents in step."

Ken Martinson
Founder of Marching.com

"DJ does it again! Band nerds of all ages will enjoy the humorous, thoughtful, and clever lessons presented in the book. Witty illustrations by Dan Dougherty add an extra level of value."

Courtney Brandt
*Author of The Line Series and
Confessions of a Teenage Band Geek*

"DJ has such a unique way of looking at what we do every day in band class and on the marching field. As band directors, we not only teach the first chair students, we (at least) try to teach and inspire every student in every chair. The lessons and the laughs in this book will help many band directors keep their feet in time and their humor in check."

Ben Harloff
*Original Blast Cast: Trumpet Soloist
Carolina Crown Brass Staff*

"DJ has done it again with his great insight into the everyday lives of all of us Band Nerds. He has the unique ability to take a new, jovial look at the situations we took for granted, the behaviors we ignored, and the personalities we had forgotten about after years of therapy. If only I had this book and these rules while coming up through the ranks, I'm sure that I would have have had at least a few less awkward moments."

__Jeff Handel__
Associate Director of Bands and Percussion
Wando High School, Mount Pleasant , SC

"Oh my…still laughing! I literally wanted to tear every other page out and plaster it on my colleagues' lockers or make it into a t-shirt. Some things about band never change."

__Amy McCabe__
Trumpet/Cornetist;
"The President's Own" United States Marine Band

Fun

Fun is the greatest luxury of our time. It's become our way of rewarding ourselves after the real "important things" are taken care of. Having fun, although we like to say it's important, is extremely underrated. Fun should be the supercharged, nuclear, cosmic fuel that can power the world towards the way we always hoped it to be. If more people were having fun, there would be no reason for hate or discrimination or any other evil. Regardless of your world and social views the truth remains: Evil is not fun, Good is fun. Fun is inclusive, loving, humorous, healing, and everything else that moves us forward. To all the people who are slowing us down...lighten up. Grab a cupcake and chill out. The world's lost a bit of its will to have fun. To me, that's dumb. I don't want to be dumb.

Treat others how you want to be treated.

It's a salute, not interpretive dance.

Every day is a deodorant day.

Never put a freshman on water duty.

Never put a senior on water duty.

"Dress Right" has two meanings.
Both equally important.

Band parents mean well.

Passion is good.

Compassion is better.

Don't lock your knees when standing at attention.

Revenge is sweet.

Careful what you post online.

Don't let the guard lead stretches.

Technology can enhance the show...

...except in the rain.

Trombone slides are not lightsabers.

**Don't worry about what's going on
in the back of the bus.
It's better you don't know.**

Live animals are not a good idea for any show.

Trumpets...calm down.

Being in charge of the metronome ain't so bad.

When life seems too big to overcome, slow it down, take one measure at a time, and subdivide.

Band Nerds
"Pay-Attention-To-Us-At-A-Football-Game" Kit

1. Fog Horn
2. Six foot gigantic trophy w/movable cart
3. Bikinis for the band
   ...EVERYONE in the band.
4. T-Shirt rocket launcher
5. Hometown reality pop star
6. Emergency Earth, Wind, & Fire music
7. A backbeat
8. A backflip to a backbeat while back'n that thang up
9. 8 gigantic drums in the front
10. A cute puppy

**Never give drummers metal sticks.
They think they're ninjas.**

But most ninjas are clarinet players.

**Band parents *are* adults.
But that doesn't mean they don't
need supervision.**

What happens in sectionals, stays in sectionals.

Don't be "that person" during the company front.

No energy drinks before the show.

Although you must focus on where you're going, don't forget about what you're doing.

If you get a flute solo...rock it.

There's something to be said for being a nerd.

Toes up...

...'cause ya never know.

Pyramids don't work in marching band.

Use a special mellophone mouthpiece when possible. It makes it easier to stay on your face.

**Let the uniform parents do their job.
They probably know best.**

Never try to make a French Horn shaped formation. It's just too confusing.

Law of the jungle:
Serve or be served.

Directors can wear t-shirts and shorts during rehearsals.

Never run with a piccolo.

Always run with a sousaphone.

**Be nice to alternates.
You never know when they'll
be your drum major.**

Earn respect. Don't demand it.

Marching Band is an art not a sport.

But if it were a sport, the drummers would win.

Make sure to respect your elders.

They need it in today's day and age.

Don't expect too much from saxes during a horn flash.

Don't expect <u>anything</u> from baritones.

Use the force.

It's easier on the back.

Practice 8 to 5 whenever you can.

But not 24 to 5.

There is such a thing as "over performing."

As cool as gauntlets are, they should only be worn during band performances.

Invest in a full length mirror.

Take what you do seriously.

But don't take yourself too seriously.

**Always make sure the bari sax player
is taller than the instrument.**

Give the announcer the phonetic spellings.

There's a reason bassoons don't march.

If you make a mistake...sell it.

Don't cut the band's funding.

It's not a pretty sight.

Wear the right color socks.

Cheese fundraisers are not a good idea in the summer.

Beauty is in the eye of the beholder.

A real piano is too much for band parents.

Don't take "pit" literally.

**Clarinets,
Don't worry. Someone, somewhere,
hears you.**

Having the band dance is cool.

Just don't forget about your instruments.

Angels don't have a favorite instrument. They love everyone.

...on the other hand.

Never serve sushi before a competition.

**Flutes,
Be sure to work out your
left shoulder too.**

Some things aren't meant to be tossed.

Hockey and band DO have something in common.

**Listen to your section leader.
Your life may depend on it.**

Bring a bigger blanket.

**Be sure to think about any
pass-throughs before running the drill.**

The performance is a celebration of all your hard work, not the culmination of it.

Don't use rubber sticks.

Balloons are not a good idea.

Go to the bathroom BEFORE practice.

On your first day, ask more questions instead of knowing all the answers.

Make sure people can understand your show.

Size doesn't matter...much.

**If a judge gets in your way,
keep marching.**

Just make sure it's not right before a halt.

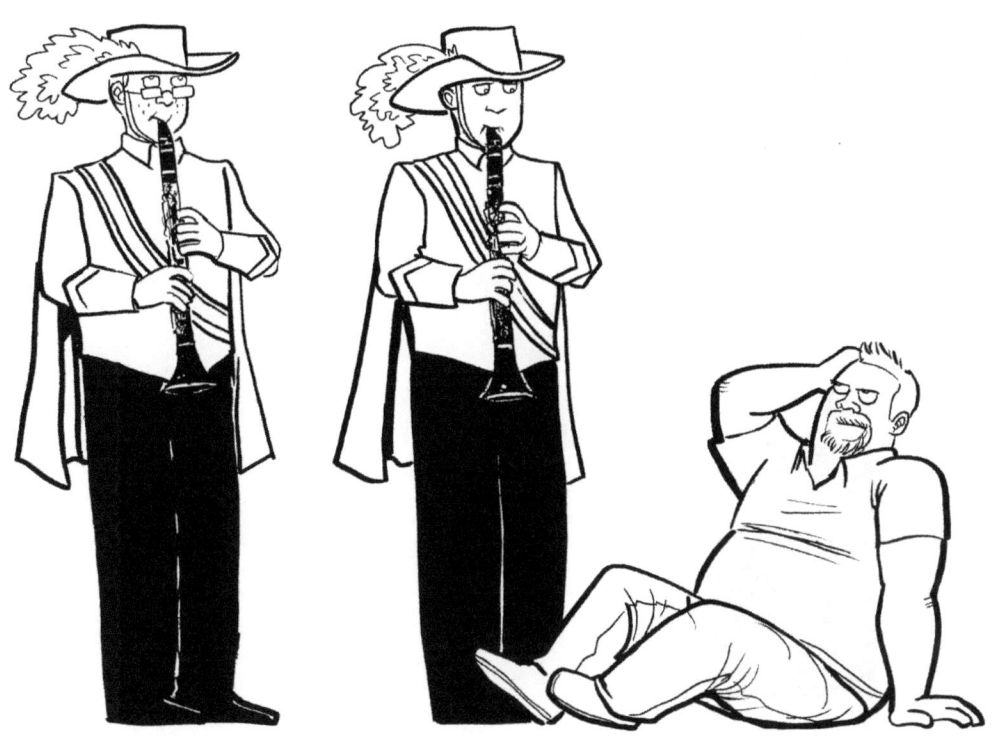

Never lick your horn before a cold night performance.

**Actually, never lick your horn.
That's just weird.**

Teach the parents the appropriate time to applaud.

**Stay hydrated.
Rehearsal in the heat is hot.**

Color guard's famous last words, "Trust Me."

**Make sure to mic the oboe solo.
They just can't handle fortissimo.**

Don't judge a book by its cover.

Judge it by its spine.

Stick to the basics at the concession stand.

If it's windy, don't toss.

Sometimes props can be too much.

Don't fight amongst ourselves.

When designing the guard costumes, keep in mind the month of November.

It's a podium, not a studio apartment.

Never use Velcro shoes.

Don't forget to turn off the mic.

**Only fart during the loud parts.
That's what the f stands for.**

That includes the audience.

The Unscalable Wall

My marching band and I reached an unscalable wall.
We tried to climb over but it's impossibly tall.
It's a million feet wide, and a billion yards up.
We tried to march through it but that wasn't enough.

There were words on the wall that were scattered about.
Words like difficult, impossible, fear, and self doubt.
Sometimes we'd feel like we wanted to quit.
That the wall was much bigger than we'd like to admit.

But we'd pick ourselves up, and break down our parts.
We'd drill in our moves 'till we knew them by heart.
The judges would judge us show after show,
The wall's shadow upon us wherever we'd go.

But when Finals arrived the words were not taunting.
The wall was still there but it wasn't as daunting.
In the end it was us that the audience crowned.
We made a wall of our own, a wall of our sound.

Have fun.

Peace with a whole lotta hair grease.

                                        See ya.

                             - The 13th Chair

A special Band Nerds thank you to:

Jessica
Mom
Scott
Chance
Meg
Kevin
Greg Bimm
Courtney Brandt
Ben Harloff
Chuck Henson
Jeff Handel
Ken Martinson
Amy McCabe
Jason Wick

BAND NERDS
Confessions & Confusion

Quotes from **The 13th Chair** Trombone Player

By
DJ Corchin

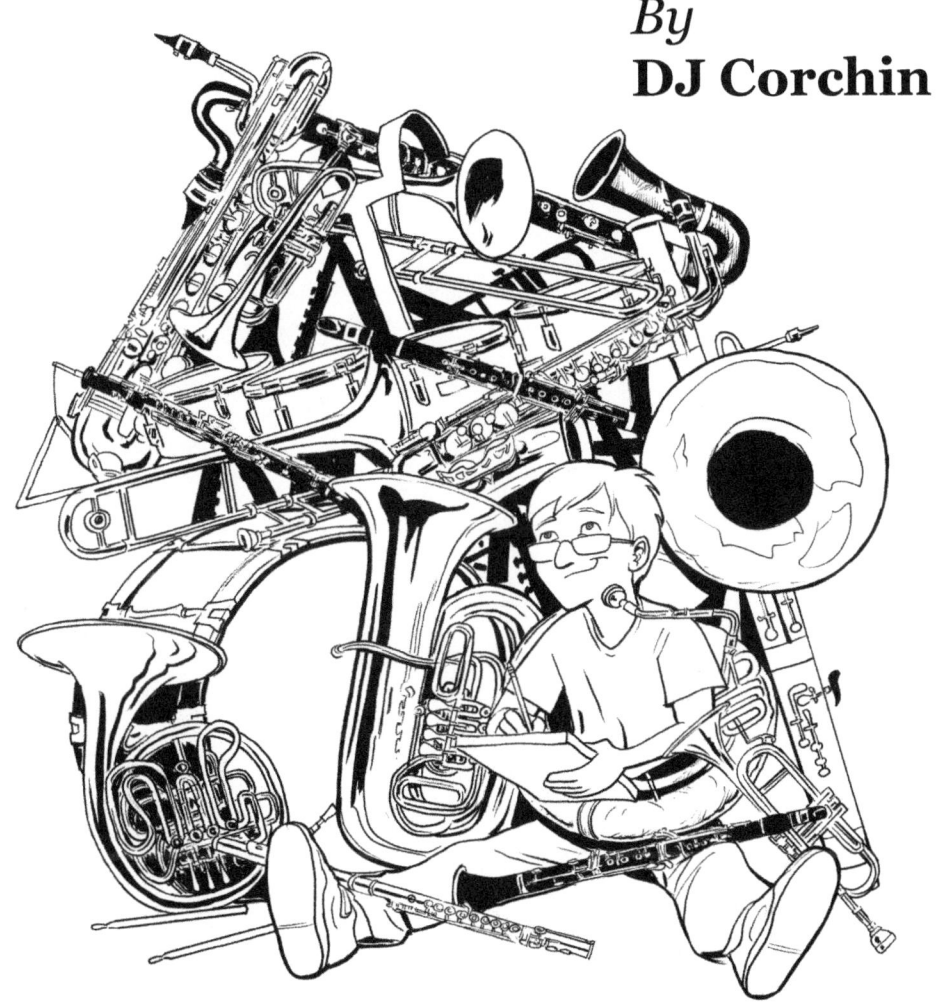

Illustrated By **Dan Dougherty**

Part of The 13th Chair's
BAND NERDS
Book Series

Belief

So often we look at someone who is fighting for music education as a passionate individual. One who thinks if their voice is loud enough, it warrants an ear to listen. They see music education as a cause to be fought for, fists raised ready for battle. But what they really are is someone who has a strong belief that the implementation of music education is not only necessary but inevitable. Their fighting is simply the result of losing their patience with those who can't see the future as clearly...or as warmly. As music education advocates, we need to see ourselves as not just passionate individuals, but as people who have foresight into what is going to happen. We may learn to not lose our patience as quickly and instead of continuing to fight, we will begin to educate. Belief is something that can't be outshouted, outspent, or exhausted. It is simply a permanent result of what we all know to be true; When music is part of our education, the world is safer and its people richer.

**Dedicated to the music teachers
who always believe.**

I often think about what my life would be like if I played a different instrument. But I also think about if I was a crime fighting super hero who could turn invisible so that's not saying much.

> Whenever we want to improve something we add music to it. A movie, we add music. Dining experience we add music. A sports event, music. Political gathering, music. But when it comes to our education system we take music away to improve it? I call shenanigans.

Life is dynamic, keep playing.

> Funny we say, "You missed that note" instead of "Those 2457 notes were awesome!"

If that piece of music didn't move you, you must be dead. If you're dead, that explains the smell.

> Some days I wish I could just hide from the world and crawl up in my instrument. Then I think about how gross that would be and suddenly the world doesn't seem so bad.

My instrument is part of me.
Literally there are bits of me inside it.

Sometimes I put a French horn mouthpiece on my finger and pretend I have an evil witch finger.

I'm gonna play the snot out of this piece you said was too hard for me. And that will be enough for my revenge. Well, I might pee on your house too.

> They say to legitimize music as a real subject you have to be able to test it, apparently through multiple choice word questions.

Sometimes I close my eyes to get into the music, then I lose my place.

> Woodwinds have so many holes in them. I don't like my instruments how I like my cheese.

Play your instrument for a baby. You'll enrich their life and feel great knowing you can play better than them.

> Let's spend 6 to 8 weeks working tirelessly to make difficult parts more comfortable, make our air control more comfortable, make our mallet and stick control more comfortable, make posture and harmonizing more comfortable, make our team's work ethic more comfortable, then when it's time to showcase what we've learned, let's put on awkward fitting, outdated tuxes, itchy, heavy, too-long dresses, and sit in either a sweaty, poorly lit gym or a too-small stage with lights that double as the faculty microwave... and make some beautiful fine artistic music.

It's socially awkward to NOT bring your oboe to a party. Geesh.

Using words to describe music is saying crescendo just means to get louder.

I can't tell you how much I LOVE my instrument. You would be really jealous and slightly disturbed.

"We are what we repeatedly do. Therefore I am a conversation where I lie about practicing."

- Band Aristotle

I'm not giving you "the eyes" from across the band because I like you. We just rehearsed 10 measures for an hour because SOMEBODY didn't practice.

After graduation, I probably won't remember those meaningful times with my friends during that math test, the team building exercises in home ec., the emotional reactions to the chemistry experiments, the personal growth I had in physics, or the physical triumph of dodgeball day in gym class. But I will remember all that I did with my music family and who I became because of them (ok maybe dodgeball day also).

Sometimes you want to practice late at night. You don't, but you want to.

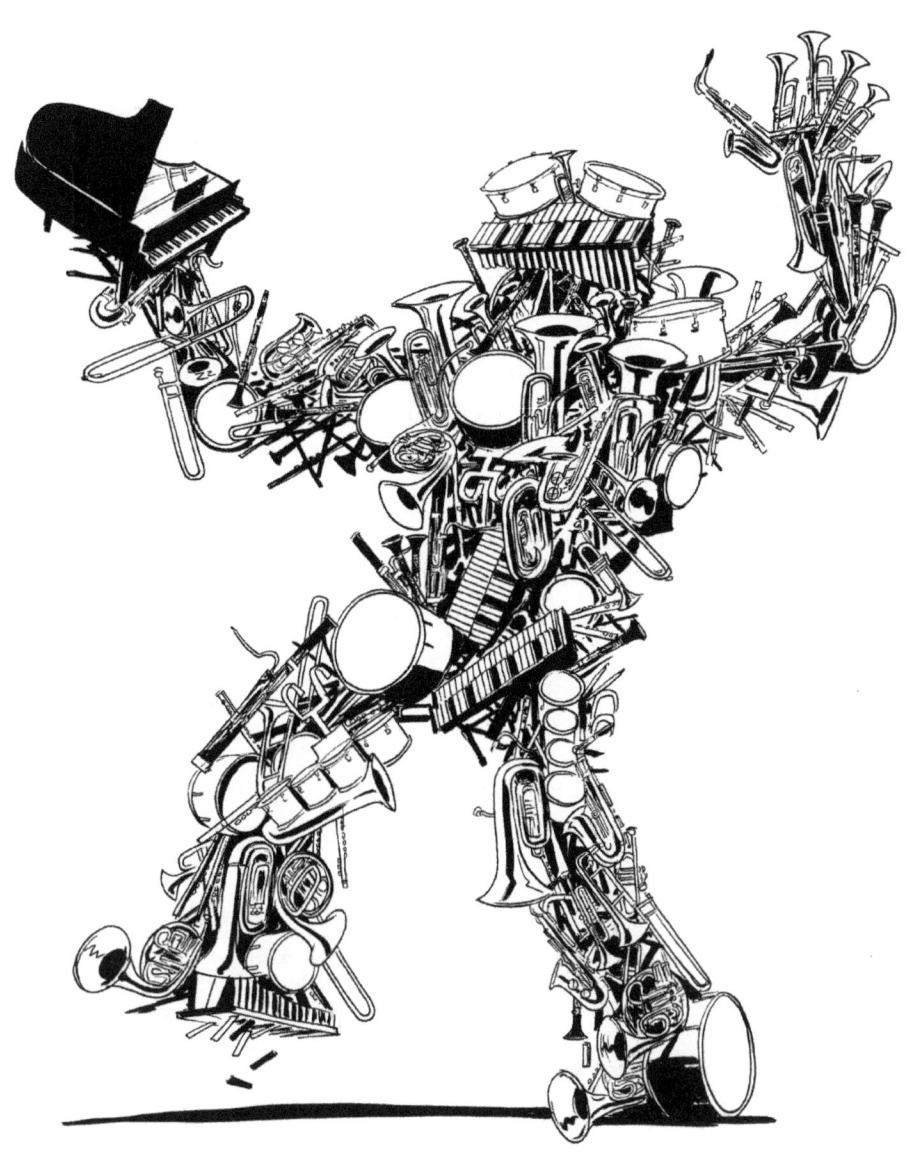

I like to think of ways that all the instruments can fit together to make a giant robot.

Sometimes in music you gotta break it down to build it up. Same goes for you.

> Someone designed the sax with a bent neck because they were so laid-back they wanted the mouthpiece to come to them…and that's how jazz was born.

I know there's a lot of similarities between music and math but it's hard to get excited about that.

> Didn't need to do cardio at the gym today. Got my heart worked out while practicing.

I can't imagine my life without music. Ok, I can imagine it, but it suuuuuuuucks.

> Treat them like students and they'll listen.
> Treat them like people and they'll find pride.
> Treat them like leaders, they'll lead.
> Treat them like musicians
> and they'll find the music inside.

Sometimes it's easy to get musical phrases & breads mixed up. Like, "I'll have a roast beef sandwich on an olive sonata."

> Sometimes life gives you an accidental.

A bad rehearsal is still a step in the right direction. It's just that step happened to be in dog poop.

When you read a book, you experience the story restricted by words. When you watch a play or a dance, you're limited to only what is created for you. But when you listen to music, you can close your eyes and be a unicorn pterodactyl on a quest to save the land of Zangor from the evil Gorilla King, Keith.

A plain note with the right amount of air behind it becomes a meaningful tone. Similar to how a booger becomes a snot rocket.

> If all you give is standardized tests, then all you get is standardized people.

Music is about relationships and emotions so be careful what you practice.

> When I need to close my eyes and go to my happy place, it tends to look like my band room.

"Wait, mom I think this present is for you."
"No it's for you."
"But it's two tickets to a show for you and Dad."
"Remember when we got you your instrument last year?"
"Yes."
"This year we got you time by yourself to practice."

> Sometimes your director forgets to cue you in and you're like "What the heck? I thought we had a deal?"

I might get lost in my music,
but I'm never lost with my music.

Want a good indicator as to how organized you'll be later in life? Look at your instrument locker. It's about as accurate as it gets.

Don't get mad at the person who no one told not to clap in-between movements. We were all that person at one point. Well everyone but me of course.

    I don't believe that the music was already there, all I had to do was find it. I created my music therefore I am ruler of it. And I shall be called Your Royal Highness.

It's not just Thanksgiving, I always think of turkey, stuffing, and mash potatoes during rehearsal. It's my motivation.

    Music is like a box of chocolates. You don't decide between the different types, you eat it all & worry about the consequences later.

"Excuse me. Do you have a pass?"
"I'm going to the band room."
"Oh. Ok then."

    The applause at the end of your show is like a giant band hug. There's always that one person who goes a little too long and makes it awkward.

Sometimes I hear someone play something I connect with and I want to respond, "I know right?!"

Your eyes are the most beautiful whole notes I've ever seen. And I've seen A LOT of whole notes.

Do you practice with a sense of fear of what will happen if you don't, or a sense of wonderment of would could happen if you?

> Music makes me dance.
> Dancing makes me healthy.
> Healthy makes me happy.
> Happy makes me music.
> Don't ask questions, it just works.

Band people are the only people to cut class only to go to another class.

> When they need it, I'll put the band on my shoulders and carry them through. They would do the same for me.

When you watch other bands perform remember our similarities bring us together but our differences make us stronger.

> Don't judge the band until you've marched a show in their shoes.

Be kind to the person volunteering to work the parking lot. The band world is small. They're most likely the parent of the person you're gonna marry.

Why do band directors use batons? Lame. I say the next time the director gets up on the podium they need to reach up behind their backs and pull out a barbarian sword. Conduct with THAT and see the emotion pour out of the band.

You might have the fancy expensive instrument but that just means it will hurt emotionally also when I hit you with it.

> Instruments don't just amplify sounds, they amplify the heart.

Love your band and it will love you back.
Just sometimes not as gently.

> No way I'm kissing you, I've seen your mouthpiece.

There is another entrance to Narnia located in the instrument storage room. Locker 19. But don't go through locker 20, that takes you to Mordor. Their music program is terrible.

> It's ok if I lose my place in the music. The dude next to me that wants my chair is probably paying attention.

To me music is life. You should get a music.

> Music means you're never alone.

Harmony doesn't mean you play the same notes. That's why it's beautiful.

Conducting should be graceful, not like you're shaking angrily. Unless you mean to shake angrily. Then you need a hug.

When you hold an instrument in your hand, suddenly you're even more good looking. Not sure how it works but it's essentially the equivalent effect of killer abs.

> People who don't understand why you would trust a fellow band member with your life have never done a pass through at 208 BPM.

Music can help you find yourself and lose your mind at the same time.

> I DO work out. It's called the practice sweats thank you very much.

Lying in a private lesson about practicing isn't the bad type of lying. It's more like not telling someone they're ugly because you don't want to hurt their feelings.

> If the music lives inside me, I would like it to start paying rent. I have college to pay for.

When lots of the same instrument play together it can sound pretty good, but when different instruments play together the music is truly magical. When will the world figure that one out?

> I played the French horn once and felt awkward like when I jam my hand in there I might pull out a baby French horn.

The sousaphone is the hermit crab of the band.

Just for fun, sometimes I'll give someone across the band the death stare during the entire rehearsal, and then when it's over and they ask what's wrong I say, "Nothing, what do you mean? Let's sit together at lunch."

> It's ok if your life is out of tune sometimes, just as long as you hear it.

If you miss a rehearsal you break a promise. If you break a promise you lose my trust. If we have no trust it's hard to love. Without love there's no music.

> If you don't get why soft and slow is harder to play than loud and fast, then it's probably safe to say you need to work on your kissing as well.

Live life like you read music. A few measures ahead but always focused on what you're playing.

> If music makes the world go round then all that stuff about gravitational forces and mathematical rotational equations was a waste of time.

The French horn is just as complicated
as the people who play it.

> Funny how people think drum major auditions are a one time thing at the end of the year.

If I had a belt of piccolos I'd throw them like ninja stars. Then wonder why I had a belt of piccolos.

I'm pretty sure music doesn't care what color someone is, whether they like girls or boys or both, whether they believe in something or someone, how much money they have or want, or how many friends or followers they have. We should all be more like music.

> Wouldn't it be great if music wasn't something you had to pay for, but rather something you could pay with?

I know music and math are closely related, but I like the music side of the family more. Why would you hang out with the "math" uncle?

> If your instrument is smelly, you might be too. Better double check...no seriously, check.

If you do music right, it will never be perfect. Just beautiful and interesting...as the best things always are.

> What if instruments were part of genetics? Like, you have the recessive bassoon gene. Would explain why there aren't that many. Yeah that explains it.

Just like music, when you lose your place, listen around you and pick it back up.

Heading to the gym. Gonna do some ear training.

"Why don't you play some holiday songs for us on your clarinet?"
"No Grandma."
"Come on. It will be nice for the family."
"No it won't."
"Why not?"
"I play Euphonium."
"What the sam hell is a Euphiniumumm?"
"I love you Grandma."

    Band is like social media. No matter what your privacy settings are, everyone still seems to see your every move.

Brass have an octave key too. It's just not very nice to put your finger there.

    Your band is like a baby. Sometimes they cry, sometimes they laugh, sometimes they poop. But you always love them.

Whether you're city, suburbs, or country we all worry about the B major scale. So don't tell me we can't find common ground.

    I overheard an oboe and violin arguing over who could play louder. I left the room as I had better things to do.

**Thor has his hammer.
I have my music.
We both bring the thunder.**

The only time I eat nachos, pretzels, and skittles
as a meal is at a marching band competition...and
sometimes on Tuesdays.

> Sometimes the only way out of life's repeat is to
> write your own music.

I once gave flowers to my drum major to tell her I loved her.
She ate them and made me use the stems to mark my spot.

> I've worked out my instrument so much lately it's
> grown pecs...and oddly enough, nipples.

Band is my core class. I take Algebra as an elective.
Gotta be well rounded.

> Band nicknames are always a little naughtier
> than regular ones.

The friendships you make in music will last the rest
of your life...or until chair placement auditions.
Whichever comes first.

> When I haven't practiced my instrument in a while
> and find myself staring at it, I swear it's staring back.

The mellophone is not the most laid back instrument.
Kind of like Iceland doesn't really have ice.

My instrument gives me warm fuzzies inside. Only when I don't clean it out for a while though.

The funny thing is, people who make jokes about
band camp really don't know the half of it. So really
we're laughing AT you.

        They say playing music for a baby while it's still in
        the womb is great for its development. So I took a
        trumpet out and blew her little undeveloped face off.

That's not a glow, it's sweat. You don't play the best
show of your life with glow.

        I will make you love me. You are my instrument.
        You will love me, I will play you, and you will like it.

If everyone was the same, the world would be like a
symphony with only one kind of note. Who wants to
listen to that?

            Be a section leader not a section manager.

The only appropriate time to fart in rehearsal is
before the first breath of the downbeat. That way
everyone tastes it.

        One of these days in that moment when my director
        makes eye contact with me right before my solo, I'm
        going to look back like, "What? Me?"

If you have to get me clothes for my birthday, the only acceptable item is a marching uniform that goes on like Iron Man.

Wait, you want me to balance AND blend?
I can't work like this.

                        Shhh I'm practicing long tones...in my head.

With my ears plugged I opened my eyes, but still felt like I couldn't see. With my eyes closed, I unplugged my ears and never saw more clearly.

                    Some saxes play to the side, some play in the center. What is that, like different forms of karate or something?

Why do piccolos split into two pieces to fit in a case?
I think it's just to patronize the larger instruments.

                    I'm sorry, I try, but I can't look at the bassoon and not think..."Whaaat?...How...How did someone think of this thing?"

It doesn't matter how much you try to hurt me, it will never hurt as bad as getting my hand pinched in my slide.

                Usually we meet our heroes and they aren't what we expected them to be. Sometimes we see our directors and they aren't we thought they'd be. That doesn't mean heroes aren't heroic, or directors can't be inspirational. It just means they're imperfect...like they're supposed to be.

Weird how some people have no problem practicing their conducting in public with their headphones on, but when it comes to dancing, no no that's too embarrassing.

Marching band is supposed to stimulate the senses. Just not your sense of smell.

> The director looks down at the boy & asks what do u want to play? The boy smiles & plainly says, euphonium. Silence ensues. Both are confused.

True friendship is when you share a look across the band after your director says something really dumb and its exactly what you texted about the night before... verbatim.

> Sometimes I feel out of my comfort zone like when I learn a new scale. But if I keep practicing suddenly life gets a little easier and I might even start to prefer sharps.

I never touch the pound symbol on my phone. It looks sharp. B'dump ching Heeeyoooo!

> Yeah I went surfing today...on the waves of perfectly locked 5ths. Oh snap!

If I could cast one music spell it would be for one good entrance. Just one! ... that magically makes me have 5 million dollars, chiseled abs, speak French, a moderately decent car like an Audi, make healthy stuff taste like twinkies, use the force anytime I want, can become invisible (with my clothes on, and not a special suit, MY OWN CLOTHES) a dog that doesn't poop, invent the fold-up trombone with cup holder, an adult-size big wheel WITH FLAME DECALS ...oh and world peace. Damn, I always forget world peace.

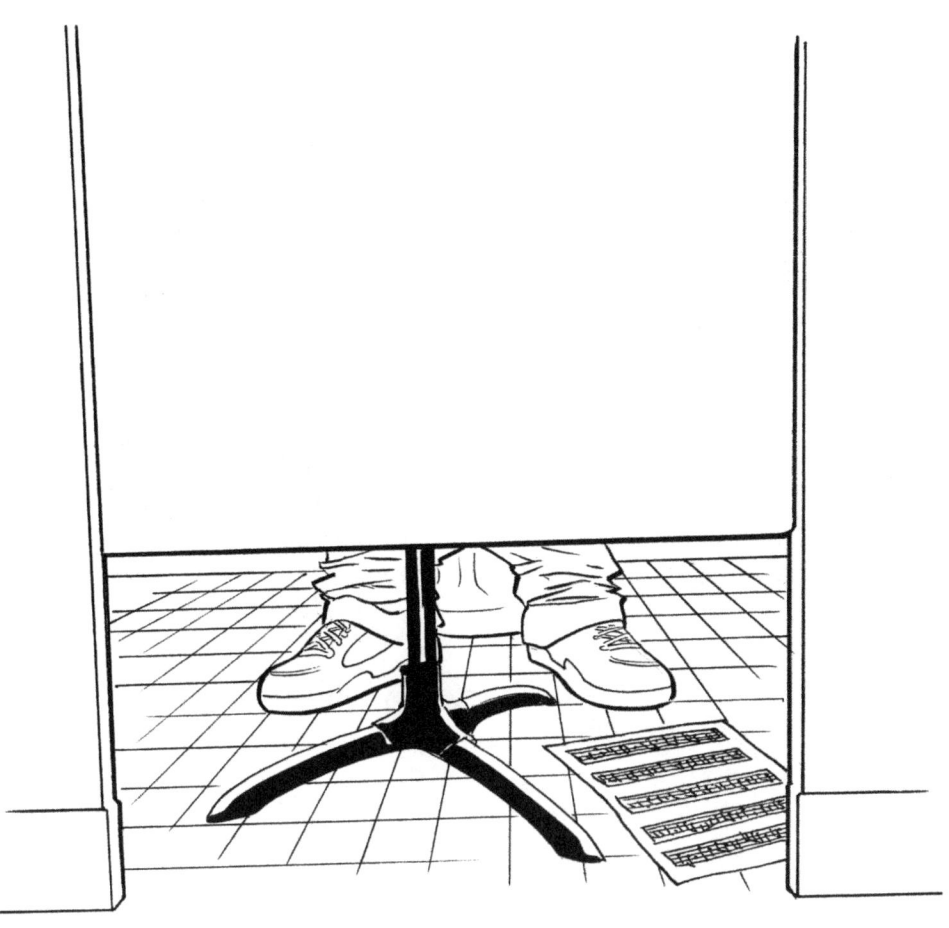

There should be music stands in all bathrooms. That way you never have to stop the joy of practicing.

When I say I love this piece I mean I have a solo in it.

        Since you're across the band and we can't hold hands, I will move my eyebrows up and down during measures 45-55. That's how you'll know I love you.

We empty our spit on the ground but in our minds, instantly it evaporates. Magic is amazing

        My instrument is like a hot dog. I don't know what's in it, but I keep putting it in my mouth.

When someone says, "You need to stop and smell the roses" I usually reply, "I can't. I'll be in a practice room all day and when I stop, it definitely won't smell like roses."

        Music should have just the right amount of silliness in it.

Music is always evolving. Musicians should too.

        I may not be able to sightread, but I can lip read from across the band.

Sometimes I think about music while I'm playing other music.

I secretly have a crush on you from across the band and really appreciate the 15 measures the composer wrote where we both rest. It gives me time to try and lock eyes with you "accidentally."

A politician threatening a teacher's job in order to get better test scores is like an engineer telling you you'll be kicked out of band if you don't play more right notes.

If I could paint like Van Gogh I would practice my music more. Ya know, because I can already paint like Van Gogh.

If you're gonna march to the beat of your own drum, better make sure you practice more than the other drums.

Great french horn players are like Olympic archers just with pitch...and deadly accurate sass.

Don't tell musicians there is math in how music is made. It's like telling them there's vegetables in the food they like.

I don't know about you but for some reason I feel more in shape with shoulder pads and gauntlets.

I don't need a therapist. Just my instrument...and maybe some skittles.

Music is a time machine in so many ways.

You're not serious about music unless you tattoo it to your face.

Play their part before you judge.

> Sometimes you sound pretty bad. Then I think about all the hard work, the hours of practice, the hundreds and thousands of dollars that went into it. Yeah, that should really sound better.

"I'm going to my locker."
"But that's the band room."
"Mind your business."

> Band people seem to be at peace with their spit.

There's a reason we're called a "band." We're in it together, we're all connected, and we wrap around open bags of chips so they don't go stale.

> When your director makes the group repeat over and over again the 10 measures before the solo you've been practicing and then ends rehearsal, it's like waiting in line at Disney World for hours only to be told it's closed when you get to the front. Noooooo!

If I sweat during my first week of concert band it's not because I'm out of shape, I'm just reminiscing about marching season.

> If the music moves you, you can ease up on the fiber.

You can pick your friends. You can pick your nose. You can pick your friend's nose. Just not during rehearsal. Save that for the concert. Then give it everything you got.

Marching band audience cheers are always more rhythmically accurate than "normies."

> If I won an award it's because I happened to. If I won the audience's heart it's because I meant to.

Next time you're bored, try staring at someone very seriously and don't say a word no matter what. Then after they get fed up with you not answering them grab your instrument and play a major scale in thirds, look at them again and walk away mad. It helps pass the time.

> In the moments before the performance, I look for laughter.

Music is plucking the right sounds from the right emotions. Like a perfect eyebrow. Pluck. Pluck. Pluck.

> You have mastered your marching technique when people with a trained eye can't tell you have to pee.

Band people are extremely innovative. Just yesterday I used my spit valve to untie my shoe.

> If you march in the same band or corps you're officially related. Like 6th cousin three times removed or someth'n. Changes your perspective on relationships don't it?

You must be quarter note triplets. 'Cause when I'm with you it seems like time is slowing down.

My doctor told me he played in orchestra & band in high school. I suddenly felt much better. Then he took out the rubber gloves.

> Sometimes I don't need an inspirational speech or motivational team building exercise. Sometimes I just need to BE with my music family.

I can't come to your concert. I have that thing…you know…when I listen to you play, I get diarrhea.

> No matter how hard you try, your reed will never smell as good as it did out of the box.

Sometimes late at night I wish I was a string player. One with long hair that can fly everywhere when I play forte on a killer concerto while my bow is shredding and catching on fire. Then I would hold it up while it was being engulfed by flames and yell, "I HAVE THE POWER!"

> I believe music education is a right.

You'd think we'd see more vampire musicians. They live forever so you'd figure at some point they'd say, "Hey I've always wanted to learn the saxophone."

> I'm not tone deaf. I'm just ignoring them.

I want to tape conducting batons to all of my fingers and then eat a lot of olives.

Ok I get the science behind it, but I still think it's weird sometimes there are holes in the keys that cover other holes on flutes.

Bass trombone players don't play trombone, they play BASS trombone.

You think, "Trumpet, that will be easy. It's only got 3 valves." Then you learn about the left hand tuning slide and you're like, "What the hell is this?"

We should pronounce "flute" with two syllables as in "fa-lutes, fa-lutes, fa-lutes are on fire!"

Every euphonium player EVERY TIME has a moment right after they tell someone what instrument they play of "am I going to have to explain this?"

There's something to be said for being last chair. You get the best perspective when everything else is in front of you.

The music speaks to me. Usually it's pretty inappropriate.

You're always just a half step away from changing the quality and feel of your relationship.

Why don't we have trees in band rooms? They produce oxygen which encourages better breathing and we can have monkeys.

When someone asks, "Hey nerd, why a feather in your marching hat" I say "It's not a feather, it's a polycarbonate synthetic resin...dork."

Sometimes I have dirty band thoughts like playing an F# in the key of Ab just to be bad. Makes me feel naughty.

Music is like chicken pox. Once you catch it, it's always in your body and it's better to get it when you're young.

My morning coffee is a session of long tones and a nice étude. Followed by a cup of coffee.

Don't let your mouth get in the way of your music.

I'm not squinting because of the sun. I have laser beam focus and I'm not afraid to use it. I'm talking to you, judges.

"You have mud on your shoes."
"I know, it was a great show!"
"We were in a dome."
"I really like marching band."

I even 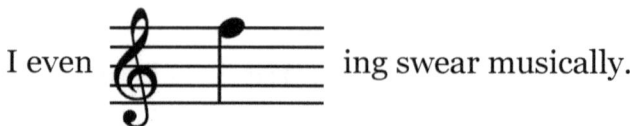 ing swear musically.

I laugh at those cartoons that have a musician playing so loud their tongue comes out of the bell. But then think, wait that would be really gross.

There's a fine line between humor and sarcasm. It's usually right between the low brass and French horns.

        People will think twice to mess with me if I poop in their bell.

When your own mouthpiece grosses you out, it's time to finally clean it.

        Sometimes I feel like the whole world's my band room. Then I realize the world has a long way to go.

If I have to clap and count, you have to conduct and do math. Hard math. Carry the one with a remainder type math.

        I use my slide spray bottle sometimes to shoo away pests and percussionists. I recommend one for all instruments.

Playing concert snare after winter drumline practice has got to be like performing surgery after a few energy drinks.

        In the future, music will be in 3D.

A unifying clef for today's musical cynic.

I like that breathing, the thing that gives me life, gives
me music. Guess that's true for mom also. Instrument
rentals were expensive.

                      Band makes me sweat in all the wrong places.

All chair challenges should be to the death. That way
when rehearsals start everyone gets a solo.

                      Make sure saying "I Promise" doesn't
                      become your "One more time."

I challenge you world, to not let your music
humor be cliché and dumb.

                      Not sure which is worse, brass mouth,
                      reed taste, or percussion breath.

If you're in music then you have ninja hearing and
can probably do one roundhouse kick.

                      I marinate my rare steak with valve oil. Aarrggg!

**Oh oboe player, just let it all out.
Let out all the air, you will feel better.**

Admit it, you have mastered the art of moving your hand like you're marking your part but don't have a pencil, even scraping your nail slightly to give that unique writing sound.

        Just listen to me play and you'll understand.

In everything you do, somehow, someway, make it special.

        I like to make robotic sound effects when assembling my instrument.

No, I didn't miss a note. It's my way of breaking up with you.

        What if the reed stayed still and the instrument vibrated? Whoa.

Practicing is a great alternative to crying about it.

    "I just need more time with you. You're always at rehearsal or practicing."
    "It makes me happy. You don't want me happy?"
    "Wait, is that a trick question?"
    "No. I'm pretty sure you want me to be happy and not angry to the point where I slash your tires."
    "Yes then. You're sounding really good at that fast part that seems really difficult."
    "Thank you! I've been working really hard at it."

**You can take a bath with a brass instrument to clean it.
Advantage Brass.
(Don't take a bath with your instrument.)**

I'm not just emptying my spit valve,
I'm dispelling the demons.

> When we're a beginner, the 6am rehearsals somehow weren't a big deal...and now...I don't wanna talk about it...need coffee.

I fell out of step because I just wanted a little attention.

> I accidentally breathed in through my instrument and now I feel kinda funny.

Take a moment to laugh. It's meant to have its own moment. Otherwise you'd be able to do it while playing your instrument.

> I feel too much pressure when someone asks me what my favorite type of music is.

I got into music education because of the money.

> Someone write a piece of music that incorporates random sounds of bubble wrap. Watch practicing increase 10 fold. No one can resist the hypnotic urge to pop.

As long as you keep your gauntlets on, you have super powers. Never take them off. Not even in the shower. You never know what evil lurks in the shower.

Music makes the world go round...then we get dizzy, fall down, and throw up.

> Got it. Conductor podium that's a treadmill. No more excuses Director.

When you ask another band nerd on a date, just remember playing etudes for each other is NOT romantic. Unless, "playing etudes" is a metaphor, then...well...

> Music is a place to go when you feel like there's nowhere else.

Do flute players fart with vibrato too? Geeze.

> Carpet in the band room itself is not necessarily a terrible idea, but when it starts to get squishy is when I get concerned.

I wish I had a harness where I could wear my trombone on my back & take it out like a big battle ax.

> Life should be a crescendo.

I'm so band I hula hoop with a sousaphone.

I love music so much I can't have it on in the background. I know you know what I mean.

> When you leave the band room for the last time it will never be the same, but it will always be there.

Euphoniums should be called mephoniums. 'Cause it's all about me.

> Admit it. You've done it too. Smelled the inside of your mouthpiece and was puzzled by the experience.

"You're 20 cents sharp."
"I have to poop."
"Oh."

> I like to practice outside. But then I realize people can hear me so I only practice stuff I already play really well.

Anyone who tells you "it's just condensation" ask them to wipe it up with their hand and then lick their fingers. See what they say then.

> Sometimes I take out my instrument not to practice, just to look in the mirror and see what I look like playing.

I heard a low note but the tuba player wasn't playing, just deviously grinning.

Sometimes I watch you play, stare intensely at your face and think... man I didn't know nostrils could move that way.

> I wish I always had a stand with me so when I need to hide behind it, it's always there.

If I don't have my instrument I feel naked. That's the real reason I practice. I don't work out.

> Sometimes I memorize my music on accident, but when I need to on purpose, I can't remember a thing.

The best player that wants to play 3rd or 4th part to learn and so others can play 1st is the section leader in my book.

> I don't think you understand this relationship. You can touch me, not my instrument.

Music puts the epic in movies, the larger in life, and the touching in moments. Usually too much touching.

> I hate when life gets in the way. Except when music is my life. Then I don't mind.

Some people's music comes from their heart.
Mine comes from my left knee.

I watch myself practicing in a mirror to practice my sexy playing face. You know, in case I need it.

The shape of an English horn looks like if you blow hard enough it will give birth to a baby English horn.

    Every time a school board wants to cut a music program, they should be required to play an instrument in that program for one month prior. We'll even give them an instrument locker and let them skip hot cross buns.

The world is like music. The more you experience the more you realize how much you didn't know.

    Music is special. Like the not quite cooked all the way through but tastes like sugar wrapped in dreams made from love, cafeteria chocolate chip cookies special.

When you're not afraid to be humbled by the music you're playing, you're growing.

    Music listens back. It just doesn't judge us in return. That's why we love it.

Can I put a repeat sign around you?

    We're the same chord just a different inversion.

You have yoga, I have marching band.

What if sections were actually alien races? Do you think their spaceships would be shaped like their instruments? That would be awesome.

When I march backwards I have buns of steel. Pow!

                       Totally want to make music with you...no wait, out with you...no I was right, music with you.

Band peeps might high five awkwardly, but a tight sax soli usually offsets the ramifications.

                     When I cry, my tears fall in rhythm. Then I remix it.

What if practicing was caffeinated? I know I'd do it more.

                       The first time you see your director in shorts you're like, "Whoa, weird."

Band moms are not like regular moms. They may not have capes, but they can definitely shoot laser beams from their eyes. To not respect this will be your demise.

              Sometimes when I'm alone in the band room, I'll stand on the podium, put my hands up like I'm gonna conduct, then think, "Huh, so this is what it looks like from up here." Then someone comes in and I act like I'm fixing the stand.

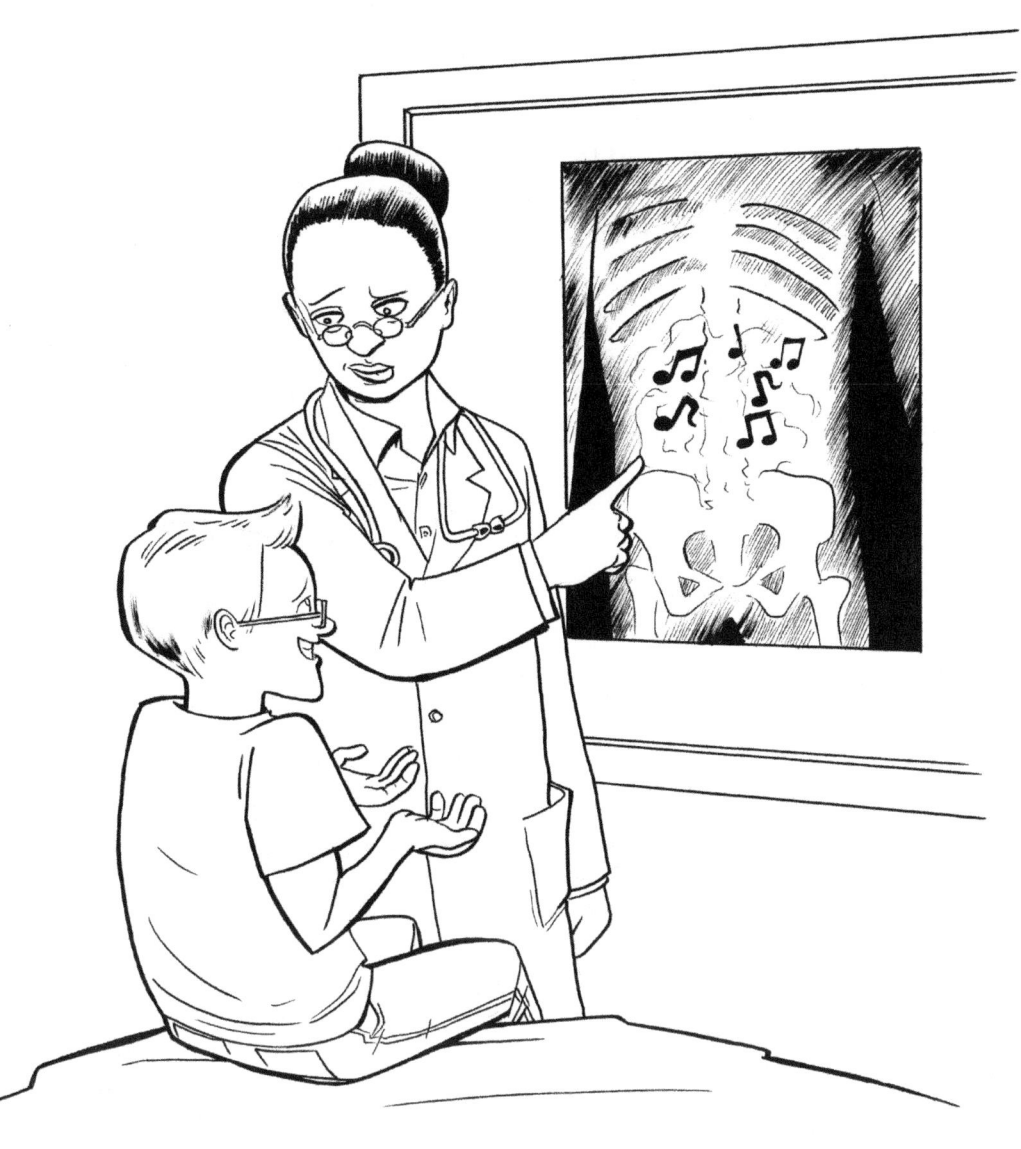

**Music gets deep down in ya.
Like small intestines in ya.**

OMG gravy makes everything better. I'm going to pour gravy all over my music.

> Marching band is something that is not bound by race, religion, economics, or geography. It is an activity that only unites us!

I would like to request we get to wear capes in rehearsal that are decorated based upon our individuality. For concerts, we'll compromise and put on our formal capes.

> I'd hug you but my uniform's too small and I can't lift my arms.

Instead of starting wars, let's start bands.

> The music world is so small I'm pretty sure you're my mother.

I hope my child has perfect pitch…and shapeshifting and teleporting powers.

> Funny how a poet and a musician can mean the same thing. And it's beautiful when they do.

It's my sectional. I'll pout if I want to.

Sometimes I'll hold my instrument case with a slightly bent arm while walking. It makes me look more muscular...ish.

Sometimes when we're having a really deep moment, I look into your eyes, get close to you in the beautiful silence, and as you're looking at me and my arms wrap around you, I start fingering through my scales behind your back.

>We go together like valve oil and valves.

I may like playing with a clarinet even though I play trombone. I may like to play with a violin even though I sing tenor. I might like to play with both a woodwind and a brass instrument even though I play marimba. Or I might even like to play with a saxophone even though I play saxophone too. It's none of your business who I play with. I'm not hurting anybody. But I am adding beautiful music to the world. Maybe you should stop talking, listen, and enjoy?

>Is it me or does fortissimo sound like a bad word?

To all the moms that help mend uniforms and hearts, move speakers and mountains, run meetings and homes, all with your boot up our behinds...THANK YOU!

>Every time you make a mistake, make sure it's a new one.

Marching band is coming. Can you smell it?
No seriously, do you smell that?

>People who don't practice and say they did are my kryptonite.

**I asked the balloon guy to make me a French horn.
He got visibly uncomfortable and slightly angry.**

You know you've reached a special point in your relationship when you're totally lost in your music, you know it, they know it, and then they bail you out with your own personal cue for when you're supposed to come in. Nice.

>Percussion I feel ya. I don't like it when people tell me all I do is hit stuff either.

I get nervous holding a string instrument. It seems like it's really easy to set on fire.

>Huh, funny. I get the same tingly feeling when I lock in my pitch.

It could be worse. It could be a harmonica band.

>Saying homework is optional is like your band director saying, "while we're working over here keep silently fingering through your parts."

If I learned ALL my scales, I wouldn't continue to grow. You don't want that do you?

>I find it ironic there is no quiet way to open an instrument case. Just smack the latch and let'r rip. Oh wait, some have zippers. Lucky zipper people.

How about instead of standardized testing we just see if you can stack stands on a stand rack correctly?

If I say I love you, will you let me practice then?

> Let me play you my scale. It's the only scale I know, but I will play it the best I can, and it's for you.

I just wrote a symphony...IN MY MIND!

> Listen, when you've been in the practice room for hours and a friend comes in and comments on the smell but you don't smell anything...take their word for it and air that puppy out.

The best music groups are the ones who love what they do every day, not just on performance night.

> Conductors, if you're going to wear a tux with tails I expect a magic trick or two.

Does the 5 second rule apply to reeds?

> I named my instrument my band director's name. It makes for hilarious conversation.

I listen before I look. That way I have the advantage.

When we win a competition let's wear our opponent's mouthpieces around our neck. (Insert primal scream now)

Did you ever notice when you look down at a bassoon reed it looks like it really wants to kiss you? Well, listen here, you have to earn this honey.

> I'm sorry BAND DIRECTOR. It IS difficult to have a pencil on my stand every day.

I'm not sure the "music makes you smarter" rule applies to all sections.

> If you think you know the most simply because you are a senior, then you haven't learned anything since your were a freshman.

Ending a phrase too early is like sticking your finger in someone's mouth while they're yawning.

> "Why are you doing squats in-between long tones?"
> "I'm aiming to hit a double G by spring. Gotta firm up. Just in case."
> "In case what?...oh...ewww."

I know my director works hard, but it's tough to think about the music sometimes when all you can focus on is their pit stains.

> If music comes from my heart, I wonder what comes from my other organs?

You can do a pull up? I can play a high F. Consider yourself served.

Sometimes you think you really know your friends and then they go and clap on 1 & 3. It's hard to reply to their text after something like that.

> I listen to you like I listen to the band. I hear it, I just think my part is more important at all times.

If band dads were the nuclear fuel of the world, the planet would be glowing and stuff would get done.

> Dear people who think music education isn't important....shut up.

You know when someone is staring off while the director is working with a different section like they were zoning out at a camp fire? Then they suddenly realize you were watching them? Then they awkwardly smile at you because you've never really spoken before? Yeah, you're friends now.

> I'm so band, I practice Holst's Mars on Valentine's Day.

Saying the instrument seating arrangement doesn't affect the band's sound is like saying it doesn't matter which way the toilet paper roll goes. It does. Over.

> New instrument smell > new car smell.

I'd be lying if I said I never thought it would be cool to have some sort of contraption on my wrist that shoots batons out like elvish arrows.

First rule of band is do not talk about band. Unless you're in band, then it's a fact we can't really not talk about it.

> You can be like my music. Sometimes I like it, sometimes I don't, but I definitely don't want to stop playing.

Band moms are the best. They take care of us with none of the guilt. Except if you mess up your uniform. Then, LOTS of guilt. Oh man, so much guilt. REALLY REALLY a lot of guilt. I'm sorry. Really sorry.

> Sometimes when I'm practicing I pretend I'm working out.

You might judge by IQ, I judge by FF.

> If we treated our words with the same love as we treat our music, friends would know less hurt and the world would not know hate.

I thought a polar vortex was the 3 feet of space around an oboe player. Bam.

> If I owned my own Magical Mystical Instrument Shop it would include French horns that speak Spanish, clarinets that are actual licorice, and trumpets that don't blow smoke.

The biggest difference between music and math is emotion...and instrument rental fees.

Euphonium players win for most affectionate instrument. They're always hugging it.

Evaluating education based on a test score is like
judging how good a musician a brass player is by
how high they can play.

> Mix grandma's feet with stale towel and
> month old kale and that's "school horn smell."

I may not be able to afford much but let me play for you
and give you the richest gift I know of.

> People don't know what they love, they love what they
> know. Which is why music education is so important.

Money can buy you happiness because it
can buy you an instrument…and cookies.

> When things are tough, I can't get to the
> band room quick enough.

What if there were playing cards for famous musicians
and directors? Pretty sure they wouldn't come packaged
with gum.

> Band people don't do stupid stuff. Except for,
> you know…that one time…at band camp.

**Don't knock my band goggles.
Without them you'd be ugly.**

Some people say that music is painted on a canvas of silence. I like to say music is breaded on the thighs of a Kentucky Fried Chicken. That's more motivating to me.

> A flute player once told me they were an artist not a musician. Fine. I'm calling you a flartist then.

No. The correct answer is you GET to come to my band concert.

> Music is healthy for both your head and your heart, just like that special someone...and for some reason a super chocolate donut cupcake hybrid.

You know when the French horn player gives you that squinted eye stare? They just decided you are now their nemesis.

> I'm getting a tattoo of a mouthpiece ring on my face. Then it will never look abnormal.

I didn't miss a note. My instrument simply misspoke.

> When I finally play something I never thought I could, I become stronger than I ever thought I would.

When you walk out of that rehearsal room for the last time, stop, look around, and remember the first time you walked into it. I bet you'll be pretty impressed with the person you've become.

Sometimes you have a rehearsal and you're like whoa.
Sometimes you have a rehearsal and you're like wow.
Sometimes you have a rehearsal and you're like, who farted?
They're all precious memories.

> Don't be the jerk who plays everything perfect but still can't figure it out.

If music is a universal language, band would be the goofy accented version of it.

> You know how when an adult would lick their finger to clean your face when you were young and it would gross you out? That's kinda how I feel when the director hands me a mouthpiece from the extra mouthpiece drawer.

Seriously? We couldn't come up with a better word than "ictus"?

> Playing music is the gift you give to yourself that others will thank you for.

Great ideas always come during long tones and showers.

> If your instrument treated you how you treat it, would it love you or dent your face?

Sometimes I get my hand jammed up in a brass instrument and walk around pretending I'm bionic.

Not a single music teacher got into music ed. because of the money. Not one. Ironically sometimes it's because they weren't making enough playing, but still you get my point.

        Thought I saw a GIF of a director conducting an 8 second slow section. Turns out it was a 7 minute video of a boring director.

An alto sax kinda looks like a goose. Actually, goose butt music sounds pretty good.

        Sometimes I get so into my music that it has to remind me we're just friends.

When I tap my fingers on the table like I'm waiting for something, it's usually scale fingerings. Minor if I'm frustrated.

        Band peeps always know where the secret bathrooms are.

Is it me, or when you look at a woodwind instrument you feel like you're supposed to find a crayon and try to make your way through the maze?

        Sometimes I make music.
        Sometimes music makes me.

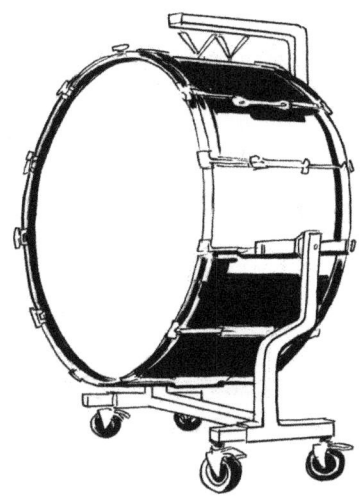

Since I'm having a stressful day give me the biggest mallet you have and get out of the path between me and that bass drum.

We should be able to customize the shape of our
instruments and mouthpieces and etch crests on them like
the knights of old. That way we will be able to tell the evil
players by the spikes and scary insignias.

> We all know if you joke about double flat
> accidentals, it's out of fear.

When it comes down to it, I'd rather have
my surgeon tell me they played a woodwind
instrument than brass or percussion.

> People are better looking when
> they make music. Fact.

As long as you're making music you're not
making enemies. Unless you're doing an
experimental piece involving slapping.

> Band means different things to different
> people. Respect it all.

Marching band is in my blood. I'm FF Positive.

> Try asking someone out on a band date.
> It's like a regular date only with wonderment.

Sometimes I play air guitar with a clarinet.

Sometimes you have to challenge yourself to grow.
The best things in life are not always in concert B flat.

>That moment on the field when you realize the seat colors in the stands match your uniforms? Power Up. Sweet.

Sci-fy makes everything cooler. Like the Quantum Oboe, Interstellar Fusion Trombone, and Autonomous Galactic Director.

>If you get a staff tattoo all down your arm you'll always have a place to write down that great idea. That makes sense to me.

When my director is humble, is when I love them the most.

>If music is the window to the soul, that makes practicing glass cleaner. Some of you need to get wipe'n.

In Austraila the toilets flush the other way, the French horns are in the front, the percussion are model students, and the trumpets have self-esteem issues. Just what I heard.

>Through music I learned to laugh.

Music is only as beautiful as the person making it...on the inside, I mean.

**You and I are hemiola.
Two different feels fitting perfectly in the same measure.
Plus we both know the word hemiola.**

Now that I think about it, there really isn't a good reason to bend your knees dramatically while playing a concert solo.

Tunekinesis - the power to bend my pitch...
with my mind.

> What happens at band camp, stays at band camp...and the internet.

I still think the treble clef was made up by a young musician doodling on their standardized test.

Having that moment months or years later when you finally get what your director was trying to tell you about life, is like when you realize how triplet rhythms are broken down. Suddenly it's not so hard. Oh....Ohhhhhh!

> Just once, they should have a marching band play in the Roman Colosseum...without the lions...probably.

"Did you gain weight?"
"No I switched to Eb Clarinet."
"Oh."
"Yeah...jerk."

> Much like all the different types of music, people of all genres are worth listening to.

If you look down the end of an instrument, you can see where dreams come from. Also sometimes bits of potato chips.

I once thought of the perfect melody. Then I forgot it.
Then it was time for cartoons.

> A true friend knows you're forgetful and grabs your music for you after you've left. Probably borrowed $20 from you as well.

I can circular breathe when I talk.
Try getting a word in now.

> Everyone in band will live on forever. Usually because of all the hidden graffiti in the storage room.

Wouldn't it be great if we made a mistake in life we could just pencil in an accidental marking so we don't make it again?

> Drum majors get so into the music they want to jump on a large downbeat. But within that split second right before, they realize they are on a rickety platform so it ends up looking like an awkward knee bend. Fierce I tell you.

If I could only find the words to describe
this music...wait what?!

> Band camp is like Disney World. Your family yelling at each other, sweating, and can be expensive. But everybody loves it.

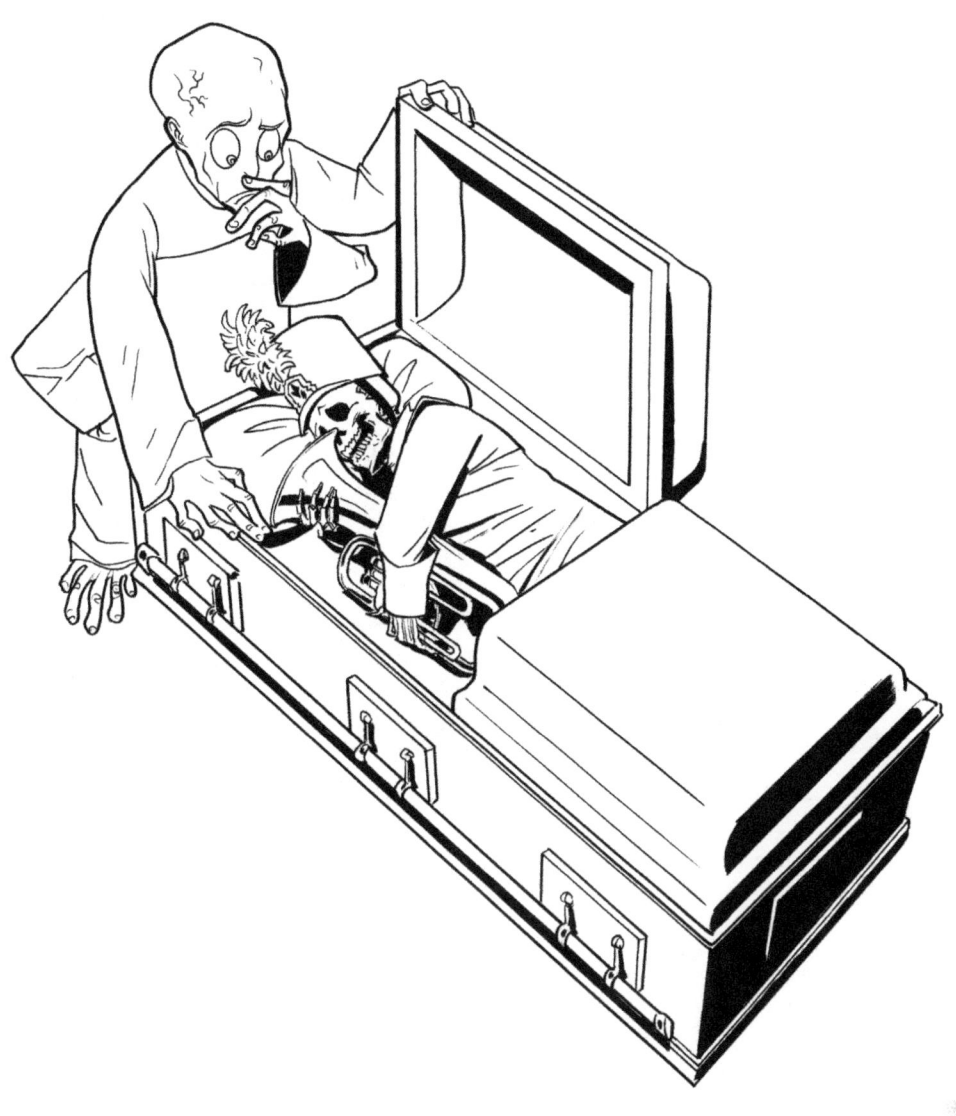

When I die I want to be buried in a cemetery where everyone is buried with their instruments so 1000 years from now when we're dug up by an advanced race they'll go WTF?!

A real leader would rather be down on the field
helping someone struggling with no one watching
than up on the podium in front of thousands.

        Having everyone at rehearsal but not mentally
        there, is like having full bars but no data.

You don't ever have to say I Love You...while I'm practicing.

        Why do instrument lockers sometimes look like animal
        cages? Are they afraid we might unleash the beast?

My instrument knows me in ways no person can.
It's awkward at family events.

        Music would survive a nuclear apocalypse.
        And Twinkies. Not a bad deal.

I can remember that performance any way I want to.
I did not miss that note. Nope, didn't miss it.

        You're hilariously musical. Figure that compliment out.

I love you. Now shut up and listen to me play this sonata.

A true friend will count the 57 measures of rest before your solo with you.

Music is a serious business. Ok, I can't even say
that with a straight face. Lighten up.

> It's not a gut. It's a perfectly sculpted
> warm air machine.

Sometimes I accidentally swear at the end of a really great
performance from all the emotion, and when I get my finger
caught in my instrument case latch, and when you make me
mad, and when I'm telling a great story, and when…

> I don't know how to spin a rifle. That doesn't stop me
> from picking one up and walking around acting like I do.

OUCH! I touched the cut time!

> It's hard to be creative when you're told what,
> when, and how to play. Improvise your life.

Sometimes everything comes together.
Sometimes it all falls apart. Just keep playing.

> My instrument will never hurt me…well except
> that one time…

Music is a great place to go when you don't want to be found.

Trombone players use their slide spray bottles just for a quick drink of water. You know it, I know it. Let's not pretend anymore.

I have climbed the most dangerous peaks. I have sailed oceans in storms that have only existed in legends. I have traveled to the very depths of hell and back but I will never, NEVER again bare the rage-filled gaze of the percussionist watching me pick up a timpani improperly. This I swear.

> If I give everything to the music, I won't have anything left for you. Tough choice.

"Digital sheet music" is a director's conspiracy.
It's too easy to not forget your music.

> When you have a bad performance, do it again, better and wiser, and you'll never be underestimated.

What good are well chiseled abs if they don't do anything?
I'd rather be able to play a double G. Ok, that's not true.

> Not knowing a math equation is not as bad as not knowing your part. Not because math is less important, but because others are counting on your part.

The more you practice, the longer you live...happily.

> Dating someone who knows nothing about music has its advantages...if you suck.

Directors assess who can play oboe by intelligence and creepy long pinky fingers. Makes you want to totally look every time you meet an oboe player now don't it?

Nobody outside of a music group can understand the true power and impact of a great story from the podium.

> What if 5 of us had instruments with special powers and could combine to form a super robot thing? Like a nerdy musical Power Rangers team. Well...nerdier.

That awkward moment when your band director missteps up on the podium and fails completely on a cool recovery.

> No no baby. It's not you. It's me...um and my section leader.

Band heaven is a lot like regular heaven, except the LESS you practice the better you get. Band hell is nothing like regular hell. You have to play in sweltering heat, with extremely painful uniforms, to a crowd that doesn't appreciate you...oh wait...

> Plungers for brass instruments are wicked cool...except if they're used.

A wise, extremely talented euphonium player once said to me, "Would you like fries with that?"

> Drummers, what if I told you the drums are going to start hitting back? Not so big and bad now are ya?

Some people just simply can't conduct soft sections. DO NOT let those people pet your dog.

We compete to test our skill, but we play to test our hearts.

> I want to live in that space between thirds that tingles slightly when perfectly in tune. It's peaceful and I'm sure the rent is cheaper.

When I'm tired of practicing, I'm not really tired of practicing. I'm tired of needing to rest in order to do other things life makes me do.

> If the world were a band right now I'd say that everyone thinks they have a solo and no one practiced.

If politics is the only possible reason you think you didn't get the part, you missed an opportunity to get better.

> I celebrated my mom today by waking her up to all 12 major scales which I now know because of all her support. This B major scale at 6am is for you Mom.

Olympians listen to music before they go out and make history. I mean I'm sure there is some working out involved but that's just a coincidence.

> Life is like music. You're meant to constantly practice because it will never be perfect.

I play loud because the music is so excited to get out of me.

Santa makes his list in score order.

When you connect with someone musically it's like your hearts are touching but without all the mess that would normally be caused by touching two actual hearts together.

> Some demand that more money be spent on devices in schools that help enhance a person's learning. I agree, buy more instruments.

I always adjust my instrument when we tune even though I have no idea if I'm sharp or flat. I consider it "band polite."

> I threw a football once. Totally threw a bullet spiral back to the ref after it veered off and hit the bass drum. Nailed it.

I'm lost in my music has two meanings, one you'll believe.

> Sometimes I don't recognize you right away unless you're sitting at the same angle I see you during rehearsal.

Be a good listener. Did you ever play great music for someone not paying attention?

> There IS a difference between playing your instrument and making out with your instrument. Most people just don't care though. Play on, bow chicka wow wow.

Lots and lots of Pixie Stix are a great way to prepare for rehearsal.

Be good to your band. Treat it well. Take
care of it and it will do the same for you.

> Be aware, practicing lip trills without a
> mouthpiece can be uncomfortable for
> those around you.

How come the object we're supposed to watch the most, many
of us from a distance, is a short stick thinner than a pencil?

> The only phrase that provides a sense of
> safety and awkward concern at the same time
> is, "Don't worry I'm a band parent."

Listen, and you might see something you've
never seen before. Weird right?

> If I don't play music for a while I feel like
> I've lost something. Like my keys, I'm
> always leaving them in my case.

Saying something is musical always has a positive
connotation. That's not a coincidence.

> I love you until the end of cut time.

Of course I believe in magic.
I'm a musician.

**My music is more than just me and my instrument.
It's more than me being part of my band.
It's the way I choose to connect with the human race,
in a way that we can all understand.**

Since you didn't mark it last time, if you miss that
E natural again I'm flicking a booger at you.

                                        "What do you play?"
                                        "Timpani."
                                        "Weird."

It's one thing to be inspired by what you do.
It's another to be inspiring because of it.

                If teachers in cartoons sound like trombones,
                what do trombone teachers sound like?

For the holidays I FINALLY got an instrument that
is in-tune. Coincidentally it will come in handy with
the extra practice I've recently been doing. Wait…

                I will provide life's necessities of water, food,
                shelter, love, and music to my child. I will also
                teach them how to stick their tongue out, burp
                real loud, and our super secret handshake.

It's a bummer when your director yells at you all
the time for forgetting what you just rehearsed.
Good thing you have a bad memory.

                You're allowed to love all types of music.
                Same rule applies to people.

I'm pretty sure if I had a cat, it would play oboe. Cats just seem kinda oboe-ish ya know?

No need to mic the woodwinds. If they were meant to be that loud they'd be built with more chutzpah.

> Ever play so loud you rattle your skull? Some people drink coffee. I do that.

It's weird if your dream vacation get-a-way is a band trip. Don't let anyone tell you differently.

> After years of marching band I'm sure I can be that awesome waiter who carries 12 trays at once. Roll heel toe!

Practicing even after everyone else says it sounds fine...

> Please wash your feet and your mouthpiece. Everyday I'm going to make you a little less gross.

Dear next greatest science fiction movie maker, please include an interpretation of marching bands in the future. I would like to see my vision of instruments made from liquid metal that change shape at the will of the player come to fruition. Also at least one cyborg evil judge to add to the drama.

> If I win the lottery, I'm buying every band kid their own instrument.

I hold my utensils like drumsticks traditional grip while waiting for my food. Pretty sure people can tell I'm not a drummer.

I may or may not have held my instrument
inappropriately a few times because I thought I was
being funny. Don't judge me, you've done it too liar.

>   Courage can be knowing you're not the best player in
>   the room but still offering your musical thoughts.

When you walk out after an amazing rehearsal,
for that moment...you're invincible.

>   If woodwinds can make their own
>   reeds then I want a smelting class.

If you're serious about music, then you'll allow
yourself to laugh when you feel you don't deserve it.

>   Band can make you grow up or throw up.
>   Either way it's your choice.

If instruments were animals I'm pretty sure
percussionists would be wild boar.

>   No my belly's this big because I've been practicing my
>   breathing so much. Pure muscle...and a few nachos.

I missed my entrance because I was
just so into the music.

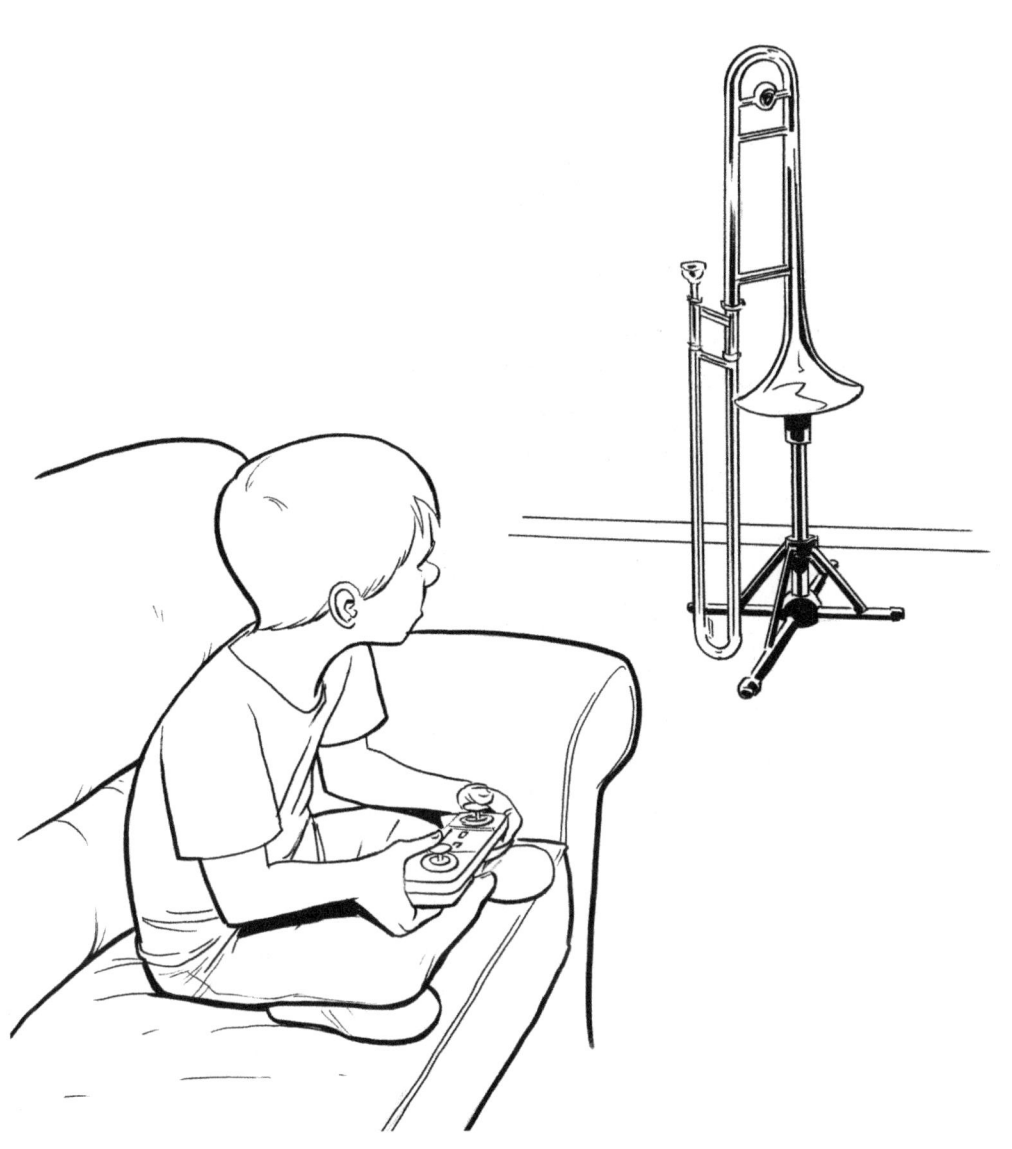

My instrument judges me.

And for my next trick I will blow air through an oddly shaped piece of metal or wood and create complex mathematical waveforms that make tiny bones in your head vibrate to trigger a sense of joy and pleasure. But the real magic will be if I can get paid for it.

> I wonder which is harder to put on, brake pads or clarinet pads.

It's not that percussionists aren't affectionate or that it's difficult to hug with a harness on. It's more like...how do I put this...they hate you.

> I live for Fortissimo, but secretly yearn for Pianissimo. Like a professional wrestler.

I have a favorite accent. It's a "French Staccato." It's like a regular staccato, but I have way nicer shoes.

> Classical Alto Saxes are like Vampires. They suck the fun out of you and then you become one. Naw, I'm just kidding. But seriously...

When there's no end in sight, stop looking and start listening.

> Why is the director always pointing? So rude.

**No your heart didn't skip a beat. I just live in 5/8.
Won't you join me?**

Is it too much to ask for a coffee maker in the instrument locker room? I'm no diva, but what is this the middle ages? Oh, and please be sure to rinse it out when I'm done. Sheesh.

> It's ok if you'd rather be playing in the graduation orchestra than waiting to get your diploma. That doesn't mean you won't run like hell when it's over.

I count rest measures on my fingers. Sometimes my section does it all together. On occasion we're still late…but we're late together and isn't that what really counts?

> I care about the environment so I bought a hybrid instrument. Runs on part air and part awesomeness.

If I were a fish I would be a musical fish.

> When your director conducts so hard their cheeks shake, think about it in slow mo.

Music is only as beautiful as the person making it…on the inside, I mean.

> Sometimes I misjudge how close my mouthpiece is to my face.

Inspiration comes in all forms. Including freshmen.

I'm pretty sure someone in band somewhere is a superhero.

I'm going to use the word "epic" to describe every piece of
music I talk to my friends about and see if they notice.

> When I feel bad I put on sad music.
> It's just one of those things.

There are some double standards I'm ok with. Bands
getting stadium practice time but football teams not
getting band room workout time is all good with me.

> Only analyze chord progressions of pop tunes
> playing on the radio with other music people.
> It's for your own good. The world isn't ready
> for that quite yet...soon though.

I like practicing with you because you understand
the positivity and purpose in my mistakes.

> Is it ironic that the tests designed to rate
> and rank our intelligence are dumb? Wait,
> what's the definition of irony again?

In the future when we all have one robot
arm I'm gonna play some mad scales.

> Are you involved with music to escape who
> you really are or to be who you really are?

Reading in different keys and somehow saying
the same thing. Music is simply amazing.

If I had telekenesis I would join winter guard and do the most amazing tricks. Probably do other stuff too.

We are not the lower band, we are another band. And
we play with just as much love for what we do as you.

> The people who study apes are the only ones who
> understand how it feels when someone calls a
> Euphonium a baby tuba. It's not a monkey!

There's a line between practicing too much and making out
with your instrument. A very thin blurry line.

> I want to live until 100.
> I've got too much music to listen to.

I've only cried in three places.
Where I was born, your arms, and the band room.

> It isn't the band directors that act like they're
> perfect that influence the most. It's the ones
> that act like they're not.

I want to secretly replace the baton with a slightly
curved one and see if the band plays any smoother.

> When music becomes a business, it ceases to be art.
> When schools become a business, it ceases to be education.
> No wonder we struggle to value music education.

Drum Majors should enter the field on unicorns 'cause on the field, anything's possible.

A section leader who thinks they're the best is like decaf coffee. Ineffective.

It's possible to look cool walking in slow-mo with an instrument. I just have to figure out how.

The only reason I cry is to sample the sound my tear makes when it hits the floor. Then I remix that bad boy.

After an amazing performance of a piece, we should bang our chests and clank helmets. Oh, we should start wearing helmets.

Sometimes I get so into my music that I close my eyes and move my head passionately. Then I go sharp and crack a note.

If I had 4 hands, I would totally play a trombone/guitar duet with myself. If I had 4 hands.

If we standardized all the music, it wouldn't be very good music. If we standardized all the tests, they wouldn't be very good tests. Oh, wait...

When you're the only one who laughs at your director's joke, don't be startled by the weird looks coming your way...that's normal.

We perform surgery with lasers, send information through thin air, and can create whole worlds with a single computer. Conductors still use a stick.

Playing your last show ever is just as bitter sweet as raising a tiger from birth only to have to let it go. You want to keep it, but you know if you do it will one day maul your face off.

> Chair placement doesn't mean much when everyone has to march in step.

Politics brings out the worst in us.
Marching Band brings out the best of us.
Less Politics. More Marching Band.

> If we had to raise our instruments from birth we would all be amazing musicians. You know, cause we wouldn't want to hurt baby instruments.

I want a world where we can upgrade our
instruments like in video games. I would add Bell
Fire Charm and Valves of Power.

> If a gifted musician teaches private lessons, is it considered regifting?

It feels more like I'm coming home for the day
when I walk into the band room in the morning
than when I walk into my house at night.

> When people tell me I can start over with a blank page, mine is staff paper.

All's I'm say'n is there is a large business opportunity investing in bus ventilation systems for marching bands.

If more people had music in their education, there would be more available sticks and less clenching.

> Talking to you is just as frustrating as trying to write note heads at the perfect angle. My computer will solve both problems.

Listen here music. It's called a staff.
So get to work and make me some money

> I love you so much that I'll let you listen to me practice.

What if you got your math grade by auditions? Like you'd have to come in front of a panel of judges solve your best math equations, fill out all addition, subtraction, division, and multiplication tables, and then sight solve an age appropriate worksheet. Still doesn't seem fair.

> Your director works out so much they look like a buff oompa loompa T-Rex waving their arms. It's hard to play soft and sweetly watching that.

I invented a new fragrance. It's a mix of inside old back-up instrument case and audition anxiety. It's pretty potent.

> Music is my life. Or is it my life is my music?
> I'm just gonna go practice and let it figure itself out.

When life gets you by your roots, try a different inversion.

If we all had rocket boots we could do drill in 3D.

Great musical groups don't hope they'll get
better, they believe they will.

> What? I'm a brass player in orchestra. I don't play for
> like 643 measures and I had to go to the bathroom.

If someone says music isn't powerful, they've obviously never
met Brett, the 6 foot 3 all-state wrestler/bass clarinet player...
or Jen, the 5 foot 2 sax player who can destroy you emotionally
in a 10 second conversation. Music isn't powerful? I have the
battle scars to show it....punk.

> I once yelled hello down my bell. Yesterday
> someone yelled back. That was weird.

Asking if music people are smart is like asking
if Yoda's boogers are green. Well, I mean...
you're in music, you get my point.

> The silence from everyone in the group after
> you realize you played something special is
> often just as beautiful.

I think it's cool when string player's bows shred as they
get intense. My lacquer does that sometimes.

> My third valve finger seems like no matter how hard I
> practice, it will always be the last kid picked for kickball.

**Turns out my instrument IS a Transformer.
But it just turns into another instrument.**

You can love your instrument, just don't be IN love with your instrument. It makes for socially awkward situations and I won't be able to take you anywhere.

> There's no better feeling than picking your instrument back up after not playing for a long time. Wait, yes there is...not sounding terrible.

Practice ripping your instrument off your face as much as you do scales in thirds. You gotta look good ya know?

> If you put two instrument bells together it's like they're kissing, but just as good friends. We're an affectionate people.

(deep breath) There's nothing worse than waiting through the unspoken hidden silence of the slight movement in your director's face after you completely blow a significant part in a piece you're performing because you didn't practice the way you said you did, you know it, the director knows it, and there's still five and a half minutes left.

> If my instrument was made out of chocolate, I would have a serious conflict of interest.

Normal people can't appreciate a whole note being played at a calming mezzo piano with a tender soft tongued beginning, released by the perfectly timed stoppage of air. Don't be normal.

> Sometimes my mind wanders while I play. It's when I do my best thinking.

Watching someone experience their first drum corps show can make you a little bit nervous as you wonder who's gonna clean up after they soil themselves.

I remember the first time a director asked me to sing my part. The reaction was like asking a lawyer to build a piece of furniture.

> There's nothing like the calmness of being the only one in the band room in-between the end of the school day and the evening performance. It's my zen place.

Air Euphonium and Air Oboe don't have the same ring as Air Guitar. See, they DO have something in common.

> It was once said a jazz piano player went crazy trying to swing whole notes.

If I could keep a marching band in my pocket I would. It would be weird when it played though. "I'm not happy to see you…just my march'n band."

> Low brass embouchures always look like they're holding back a belch. Then they play… coincidence?

Try whispering "forte" to yourself a couple times. Weird right? Now look around at the people staring at you. Weird right?

> Yes, I admit it. I conduct the pop music on the radio. Too bad I sometimes can't give a cut off.

**Underneath the podium is a stairwell.
I just know it.**

Ok make up your mind. You either want no talking at all,
or you want me to help my section get better. But you can't
have your cake and eat it too...wait you have cake?

> Sometimes your band director tells the perfect story
> at the perfect time and powerful things happen.

If you had a tuba and oboe player switch instruments and asked
them to play double quadruple f, I'm pretty sure the oboe would
blow up. The instrument, not the player. Although...

> Am I the only one that has dreamt about saving the
> day during a bank robbery using my instrument?

Why all the blah blah and yak yak yak?
Can't we all just play together?

> If aliens came and visited our planet which
> would you rather have them meet, the band
> or the football team? Just say'n.

Went to the gym today and bench pressed like two
tubas yo. And not those wussy tiny F tubas either.
I was all Bb horns baby.

> Funny how the only ones who ask to prove the
> link between music education and higher level
> thinking are the ones who had none.

**It finally happened.
You played so loud...you pooped yourself.
Not easy to do on Marimba.**

When you break up with someone I recommend an English
horn playing a soft melody in the background while you
do it. It eases the tension by taking their mind off of being
dumped and onto "Is that an English horn? What the…"

> Does one wrong note ruin the melody or
> create something more interesting?

You meet someone and you're like whoa they're totally
awesome, I'm in love. Then they pick up an instrument and
kill it, then you're like whoa they're outta my league. Then you
practice harder for the wrong reason, but you're ok with that.

> I'm just saying if they want us to sit at the front of the
> chair maybe they shouldn't make the seats so big?

My love for you is unconditional.*

> You know when you have eye crust first thing in
> the morning? Sometimes I feel my instrument
> has the same thing when I first take it out.

Please don't tell me you have perfect pitch,
it's like telling me not to hit the red button.

> When the competition seems too big for your
> little band remember the competition exists
> because of you. Not so big now huh?

*Does not include holding, trying, or
breathing on my brand new instrument.

**Sometimes people say they know more than me.
That's ok, I can play my instrument on a unicycle.
Plus their momma's ugly.**

Owning a bassoon is like owning a pool cue. You don't really tell anyone about it, but when it's the right time, you're a badass when you take it out.

> You may not notice the Euphonium, but you can feel when they're not there. Same goes for when they're playing.

I went to the scariest haunted house tonight. It was actually a regular house but no one was involved with music. Ahhh!!

> The real competition is to see how much you can eat from concessions to the stands. Challenge accepted.

You might live in a world where music isn't important, but it's the wrong one.

> When you rock that duet section where you're playing with someone across the band is like when two different parts of the world find common ground and something wonderful happens.

Your director may yell at you to clap on 2 & 4, but we all know what they're like in the club.

> Sometimes I place my stand at 45 inches high at 86° so the director can't see me put my head in my hands & close my eyes.

I'm not tapping my foot loudly, it just fell asleep during rehearsal. What's your excuse?

Directors should conduct more with their eyebrows, except if they have a unibrow. Then please don't do that.

The only thing leadership has to do with you is whether or
not you realize leadership is about everyone else but you.

                Playing bass as a second instrument automatically
                makes your first instrument cooler.

This one time, at band camp... I rocked the crap out of
my part, had a killer sectional, perfected our show, and
got a standing ovation during our first performance.
Put that in your joke and smoke it. (Don't smoke)

                You can't have harmony without two notes.
                Funny how the same is true for dissonance.

The same urge that makes me straighten
paper clips occurs when I look at a treble clef.

                Music people dirty jokes tend to be dirtier
                than normies' dirty jokes. Ironically it's
                because we're more mature. Diarrhea.

Imagine if we were rewarded monetarily by the number
of lessons we learned. Pretty sure music teachers
would be the most valued occupation in the world.

    No I didn't get in a fight. I just get really excited when I salute.

If they can make a crazy straw why can't
they make a crazy flute...oh, wait.

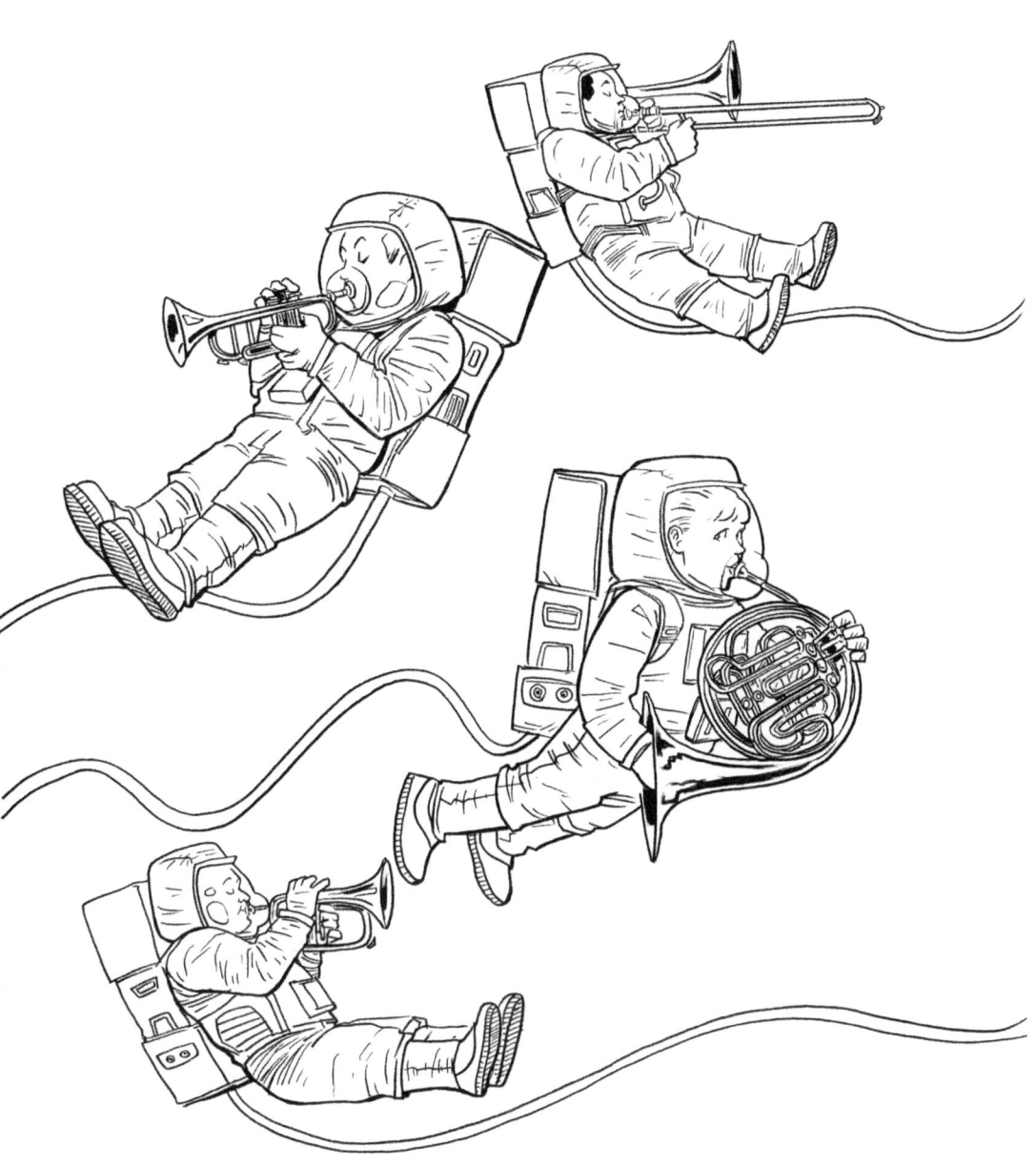

If I play my instrument in space will I move backwards?

Band is hilarious. I'm serious about that.

> "That sounded better in my head."
> "Then we know what the problem is don't we?"

Sometimes my mind wanders to something inappropriate during the slow serious parts…but that somehow makes it appropriate.

> Give the gift of music. Better throw in a card too or else they'll think you're cheap.

"Hitting something musically is beautiful," says the percussionist. So the next time you punch someone in the forehead be sure to do it with musical integrity. Then yell, "How do you like my art?"

> It's the absolute best when you need a little inspiration and your band director comes through.

Sometimes I sit down at the piano and start playing then realize I don't know how to play. But I don't stop.

> I will always be there for you, unless I have rehearsal.

You know that moment when the waves of two notes coming closer and closer in tune suddenly stop, and all you hear is one calming pitch? Yeah, you're that.

If I go to a comic convention will my band nerdiness and comic nerdiness cancel each other out like two wave forms matching opposite amplitudes?

On days I feel ordinary, music makes me feel special.

        Someone once told me music heals all wounds. That person obviously hasn't had their hand caught in their slide.

I play so aggressively when I'm hungry.

        The irony is if we cut music programs to pay for more math and science we end up with less scientists and engineers. Well, good ones anyway.

Imagine if we got paid to dream instead of encouraged to forget them.

        When you make fun of someone because of your own insecurities it's like when your director is lost in the score and stops the group only to criticize "something they heard."

I still think we should combine science and music into one superclass. Imagine the evil genius that could come from that.

        Sometimes I practice really angry and play the snot out of that sweet, soft melody.

We don't need weapons, I can blow you away with my music.

**A toast to the notes that only use one hand to play.
You allow me to scratch when I really need to.**

Playing barefoot just makes you more
"artsy" ya know?

> Sometimes I just go crazy with my instrument and play whatever random noise comes to mind just to be silly.

Imagining the world without music is like having to eat raw brussel sprouts while doing calculus in a beige room after you just stubbed your toe. It sucks.

> It's pretty hard to create music and not feel like you're moving forward in some small way.

"Tell me you love me?"
"I can't. It's beyond words. I can only
 describe it by playing for you."
"Better practice then."

> Secretly rehearse a piece you're going to play later in the year. Then after the group reads it for the first time ask your director if they have anything challenging.

Music people come in all different sizes,
but our hearts are always large.

The best thing about practicing is being proud of YOURSELF.

I wish my school horn case had more secret hidden compartments where I might find a magical trinket from bands past.

I will fight for music! I mean, not like a real fight-fight.
I'm more of a fight with my ideals classical musician
type soooooo, I've never actually been in a fight. Saw
one once though. No, no, that's a lie too.

> Music is a medicine no pharmaceutical
> company can profit from. Unfortunately
> neither can musicians.

The room where music is taught needs to
be the safest place for everyone.

> What if instead of giving someone the middle
> finger you played an F concert exercise?
> Seems less confrontational.

The band doesn't play music for the football team.
The football team plays football for the band.

> Next time my director is just freaking out on the
> podium, I'm going to simply get up without saying
> a word and place a cupcake on their stand.

Others can help you sound amazing.
But only you can make yourself a musician.

> I am a doubled up 6th chair player. I will rock
> the snot out of my parts and you will love what
> the 6th chair doubled up player has to offer.
> Then we will all go for pancakes.

If people can look like their pets, can they look like their instruments?

When I get in an argument, and I mean a really big argument, sometimes I'll take out my horn and play something really loud then rip it off my face just to emphasize my point.

> Of course my test scores are higher because I do music, you don't get multiple choice in an audition. You learn you gotta come to play baby.

Having a nose ring while playing the tuba has got to be the brass equivalent of a sizzle cymbal.

> Band drama is more dramatic than regular drama. It has a soundtrack.

Not good at emotional facial expressions while playing? Then just let the music do the talking. Don't let your face screw it up.

> Just when you think you sound awesome, you burp up Mountain Dew.

The door to the band room being locked when you really need some "band room time" is like when you wake up on Christmas and there is an electrified booby-trapped 9 foot fence surrounding your presents.

> Sometimes I don't like the music we're playing in band. Then I get a solo and it's suddenly not so bad.

I've worked so hard on lip trills I can now bench press with my face.

If you marry me, you marry the band. Except
the tubas. You don't have to marry the tubas.
I wouldn't wish that on anyone.

                        Is it me or do oboes look like tribal weapons that
                        blow poison darts? Note to self, be nice to oboes.

I once met a flute player who could blow out one
candle surrounded by ten others. She was like
an airflow sniper. Too bad she couldn't be that
careful with my heart (...tear).

                        Sometimes I think high notes are scary,
                        but then realize your face is.

If I'm crying it's only because someone scratched
my instrument. NO OTHER REASON!

                        Woodwinds use a delicate screwdriver to
                        fix their instruments. Brass use a hammer.
                        That's a metaphor if I ever heard one.

Let's build a time machine and go back. You can't
change your instrument, but you CAN change your
hairstyle. In fact...I insist.

                        I'm just say'n, baritones are traditionally
                        known for not being great colorers growing
                        up. They tend to eat the crayons.

I wish I had a professionally built practice room at home. Not to practice, just for the quiet. Life is loud.

Never pack a metronome in your carry-on luggage
without pulling the batteries out first. Bad scene.

> Sometimes I try to balance my music stand perfectly
> in the center instead of tightening the screw at the
> bottom. It keeps me occupied during rests.

I hope I'm half the man my band director was.
Band Directors don't have time to work out that much.

> I wish I could be a conductor while walking around.
> I'd give so many people cut offs and never cue them
> back in. Except for you…you can come back in.

Love the epic breakdowns in rehearsal where you have no
idea what happened, who started where, and everyone just
laughs and starts over.

> I like practicing with you because you understand
> the positivity and purpose in my mistakes.

I know I come off all big and bad, but secretly, between
you and me, I sometimes wish I sat in the front row.

> If I have to sing my part in rehearsal to get better, then I think
> it's only fair the singers learn to play their parts to not suck.

Do you have to be really smart to play the oboe?
Or does playing the oboe make you really smart?
Seriously, what the heck?

I blare wind ensemble music out of my car while driving with my sunglasses on and top down just to prove I'm better than you.

The benefit of being in the back during rehearsal is that
each day you can scan everyone in the group consistently
reevaluating who you would or would not date.

>	Staying in the practice room when you don't feel
>	like playing is like being in an empty relationship.

I love when I listen to a piece of music and
smile because of the memory it brings up.

>	They might be able to make a computer sound
>	like a real musician, but they'll never be able
>	to make it smell like one.

Your talent may get you there, but your
choices will keep you there.

>	If everyone stepped on the gas at the same time
>	there would be no traffic. Similar to if everyone
>	believed in music education at the same time except
>	instead of traffic it would be war, poverty, and hate.

For anyone who has lived with music
knows the baton is really a magic wand.

>	Music helps you be courageous. That's why
>	you listen to it during the bad times.

Dance and art get you the visuals, literature the specifics,
and music the soul. Everything else gets you grades.

To the person that designs concert white dress shirts…you're not helping.

When you find someone older or younger than you that had your same director it's like you're suddenly from the same bloodline.

> Sometimes you may need to use your personal mute. Not because people don't want to hear you, but maybe they just need to hear you a little less.

If every band and orchestra had each member write a poem, collect and bind them in a book to be placed in a library with others from all over the world, it very well might be the most beautiful and insightful place on earth.

> Clean your instrument out often otherwise people will think you fart when you play. Percussion you have no excuses. You did it.

I'm going to build Band World. It's just like Disney World full of enjoyment and wonder, it just won't make any money.

> Going through your first chair placement challenge is like your band bar mitzvah.

When you find out someone plays the same instrument as you, it's kinda like meeting an actor that plays a relatable character and assuming they understand your life...except they do.

> When I lose something I fill the space with music and suddenly it doesn't seem lost at all.

**Leave it all on the field. Except your clothes.
Please take your clothes with you.**

Your director isn't perfect. Nor should they be. That's the selflessness of teaching. They give you their wisdom and mistakes.

> I think directors pick their noses with their batons. No other reason to bang the stand that hard.

The farther apart we are the more phasing affects our relationship. Let's have a common point to focus on and we'll get in sync.

> When you catch a look with someone else in the group while performing and smile with your eyes it's like an unspoken musical hug.

My instrument locker is like my inbox without a search feature. If it's not on the top, it's gone forever.

> If you always listen to people who tell you to play it differently, than you're always an artist who only creates someone else's art.

I still remember the time I opened my first instrument case. My eyes widened, my mouth watered, and I couldn't help but think, "What the hell is that smell?"

> I admit sometimes I play on the percussion equipment knowing it makes them mad.

"Honestly, I practice in the bathroom for the acoustics,"
"You play piano."

Whoever can play the highest note can marry me.
BUT, it has to be with great tone. Otherwise no deal.

> I've always heard a music person will end up curing a serious disease. I believe that cure will be found growing in a tuning slide somewhere.

I choose to listen. You should too.

> The reason trombone players sometimes wear velcro shoes is because their spit valve gets caught in their laces. Not because they don't know how to tie a shoe...ok, it's a little of both.

Sometimes I write something and think it is the dumbest thing I ever wrote. Then I play it again the next day and it's genius. Then one more time...it's dumb again.

> You know how to be able to play your instrument faster? Flame decals.

I'm pretty sure French horns were designed by the same person who created the Chinese finger traps. I may or may not have a horn attached to my wrist right now.

> Brass players, a pelvic thrust does not make you player higher or louder. String players...it might.

I've finally identified the "school horn" smell.
It's either the trapped souls of lost alternates or
forgotten sour cream & onion pretzels.

Hey where did you're creepy long
fingernails go? Nice new reeds though,
didn't know they came in packs of ten.

>I'm sorry. I know I'm a brass player, but the Marimba just looks so fun. It's like when you were four and that cool aunt got you the seven key xylophone in multiple colors. Way more awesome than the weird uncle getting you that fake transformer "change-o-bot" thing.

Write a love song for someone and watch them fall head over heels for you. Just don't play it on your instrument. Doesn't seem to have the same effect on a bass clarinet.

>If something accidentally flies out of your director's mouth and onto your leg during a concert, don't panic. Think happy thoughts and hope it doesn't start to smell.

If celebrities started wearing sousaphones as an accessory, would you wear one? I would, except that was SO last year.

>Ok, when you have to "dance" while playing, move your whole body. Just don't bend at your waist and wiggle around, you look weird. Like awkward cousin weird.

At first I think it's gross when my instrument tastes like potato chips…but then I crave potato chips.

If you grow a beard keep it under control. No one needs to wonder where the mouthpiece goes.

If you put different accent and dynamic markings over
the words "I love you" each time you say it, it makes it
more tolerable. Try staccato I love you. Much more fun.

>   Great tone starts with great air, oh and
>   removing all cleaning tools and supplies
>   from within the instrument.

Sometimes during really long rests, I play
imaginary connect the dots with the dirty spots on
my instrument to pass the time.

>   I need someone more stable, not some
>   wobbly music stand I can't trust during a
>   solo. Know what I mean?

I have seen the boogie man. He's in the hat box room.
He gets free rent during concert band season.

>   The day before the big concert, everyone dye your
>   hair various shades of purple. The band will look like
>   a giant bruise and you can call it performance art.

The best way to get someone to listen to
your music, is to listen to theirs.

>   Music is about inclusion.
>   If yours isn't, it's not music you're making.

**We have a choice of what we teach our children.
Choose wisely.**

Believe

Peace with a whole lotta hair grease. See ya.

- The 13th Chair

Special Thank You

Jessica
Grae
Scott
Mom
Meg
Ken Martinson
Scott McCormick
Music For All

The Marching BAND NERDS AWARDS

Nominations from **The 13th Chair**

Written By
DJ Corchin

Illustrated By
Dan Dougherty

Part of The 13th Chair's
BAND NERDS
Book Series

To Ken

Tradition

There are so many great traditions in music. They connect us with our past so that we can remember our journey. They can make us feel safe as we know that whatever happens, they will always be there. There's comfort in knowing that we can always fall back on the traditions of our musical culture. However, the inherent problem with Tradition is that it implies things need to always be done the way they've always been done. Often the only reason given is, "Well, it's tradition." I believe that when Tradition is the only reason for having itself, it's time to move on. There should always be purpose in what we do. It's how we move forward. In some cases, Tradition is used as an excuse to exclude. That's where we need to step in. If you don't believe a girl should be Drum Major simply because of tradition, not only are you wrong, you're in the way. When traditions get in the way of progress they are no longer traditions, they're obstacles. Don't be an obstacle. That never turns out well ;)

And the award goes to…

Most Intense Saluter

Bassoon Participation Award

Highest Flash

Award For Most Consecutive Performances Without Cleaning Their Uniform

Loudest Trumpet Award

Softest Trumpet Award

Loudest Flute Award

Most Exaggerated Story About Almost Dying On The Field

Most Intense Pass-Through

Best Player According To Their Own Parents

"Gets It The Most" Award

Best Stick Trick

One year ago...

Most Improved Player

Current year

Best Use Of Instrument

Most Organized Instrument Locker

Most Innovative Use Of Technology

Most Creative Use Of Sectional Time

Largest Spit Pool

Largest Spit Pool By A Woodwind

Most Courageous

Most Spectacular Plume

**Humanitarian Award For An Invention
Eliminating A Trombone's Blind Spot**

Straightest Company Front

First Clarinet Section Ever To Be Heard

Award For Knowing The Most About Music Theory, But The Least About How Much People Care About Knowing The Most About Music Theory

Most In Need Of Paper Clips To Straighten

Most Hours Practicing Marching

Highest Drum Major Podium

Oldest Drum Major Podium

Most Improved Flag Work

Least Improved Flag Work

Fastest Person With A Tuba

**Person Who Practices The Most
But Needs To The Least**

Best Drill Written For Oboe

Most Overdone Practice Wear

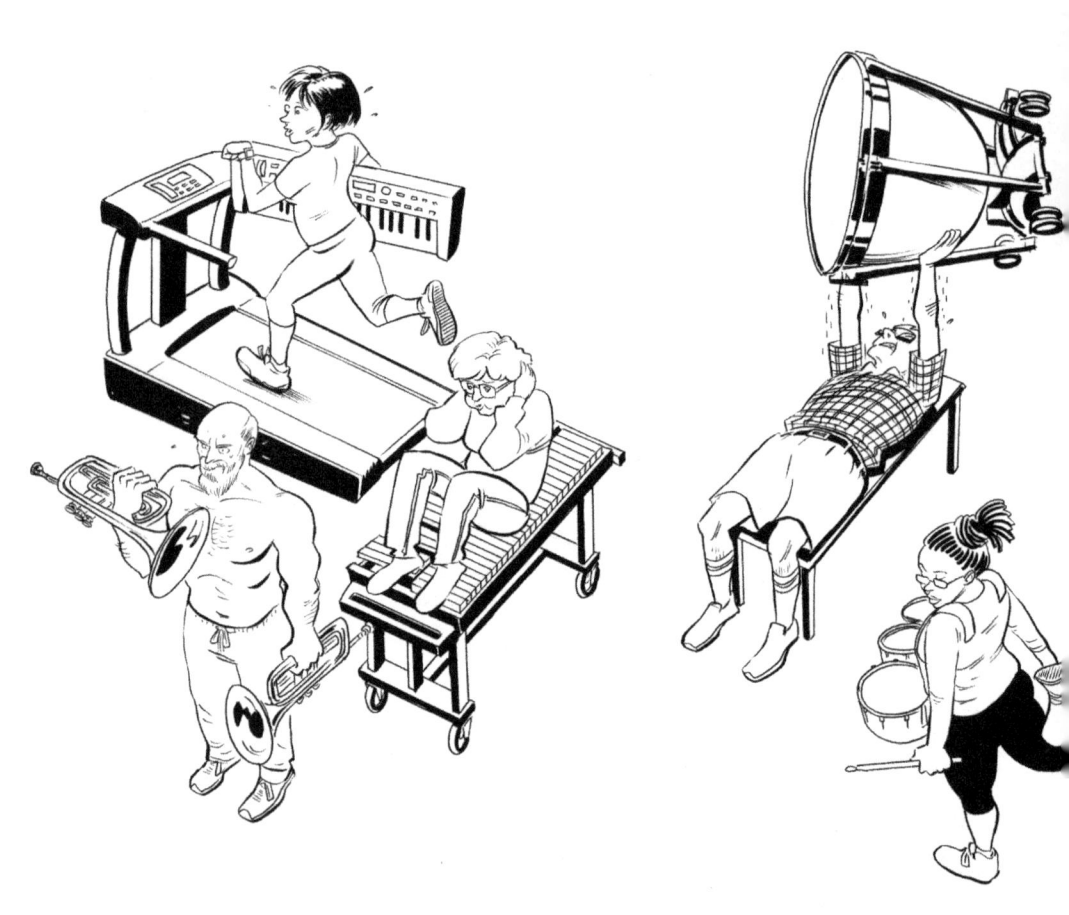

Most Difficult Pit Crew To Qualify For

Most Souped-Up Pit Vehicle

Most Flexible Flute

Best Example Of "Just Keep Going"

Hottest Practice Surface

**Most Consecutive Days Wearing
Black Jeans And Old-Timey Paperboy Hat
In 90 Degree Plus Weather**

Most Texts Sent During Rehearsal

Best Solution For The Perfect Horn Angle

Best Timed "I Needed That" Conversation In The Band Room After School

**Designated Instrument To Be Left
Behind In Case Of A Fire**

Best "Show Face"

Longest Time Standing At Attention

Most Envious

Best Fort Builders

Parent Who Always Has A Truck Available To Borrow, But Is An Accountant

Best Uniform Parent Team

Best Distance Keeper From Bad Breath

Biggest Knee Bend Before The Big Hit

Worst Bus Packing Job

Director Who Loves Technology The Most

Most Reflective Director Sunglasses

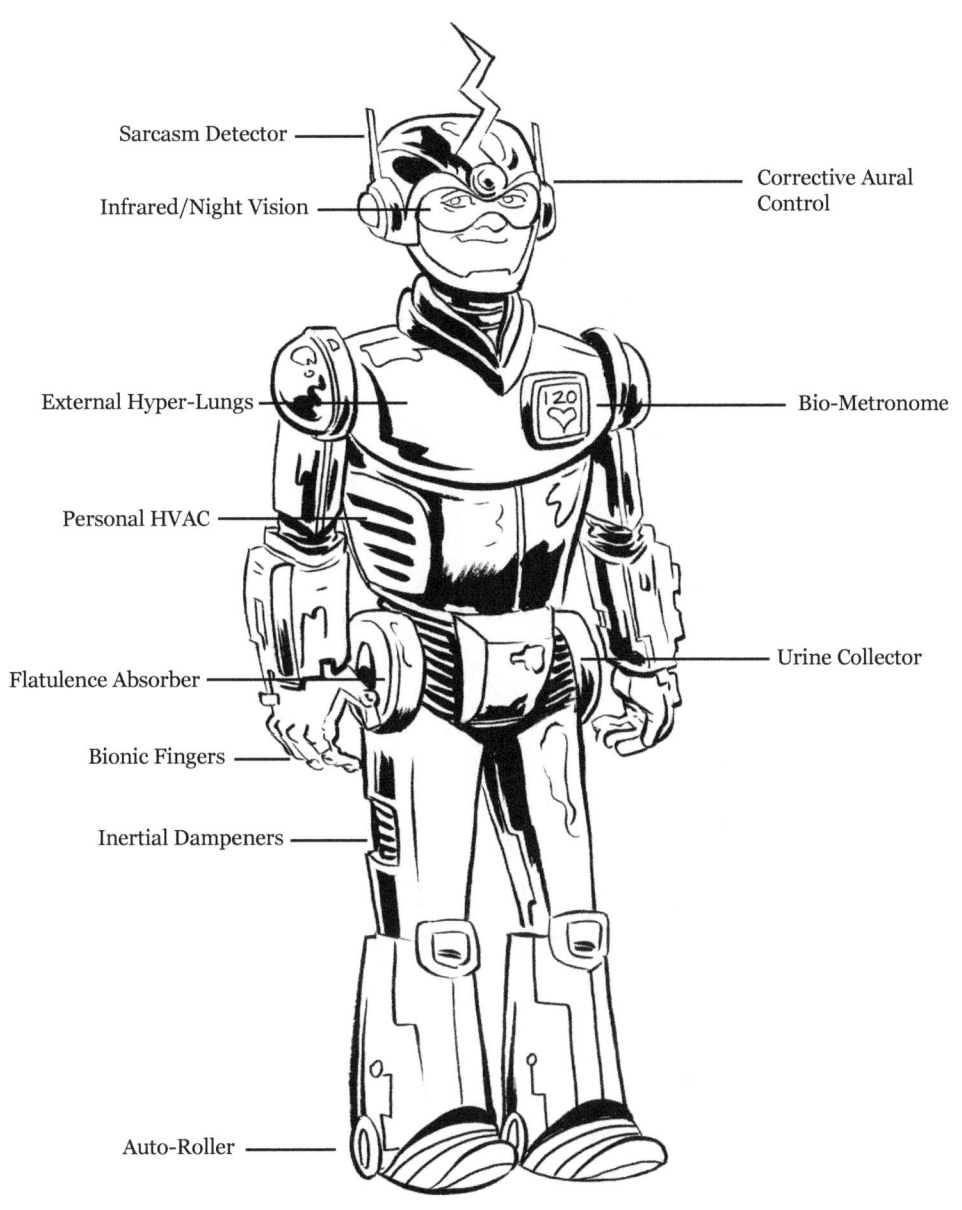

Best Uniform

Best Boom That Shakes The Room

**Most Upset That Someone
Called Star Wars, Star Trek**

Most Amount Of Props

Best View

Most More Knowledgable Than Any Judge

Most Intense Counter

Most Likely To Star In Their Own Band Indie Film

Best "If You Miss Your Spot Again And We Have To Run It One More Time I'm Going To Kill You" Face

**Award For Person Who Already Assumes
They're Going To Win An Award But
The Season Just Started**

Best At Being Able To Spin Anything

Most Frequently Gets The Sousa Case With The Broken Wheel

Most Acrobatic Solo

Most Overzealous Sound Designer

Least Complicated Show

Toughest Sax Player

Most Mallets Used In A Show By One Player

Best Children's Band Book

Calmest Pre-Show Ritual

Weirdest Pre-Show Ritual

Actual Flight Achievement

Best Use of Saber

Latest Time Returning From A Competition

**Largest Step Size
1 to 5**

Stupid Stereotype Destroyer Award

Best Dreamer

Best Place To Be

**Peace with a whole lotta hair grease.
See ya.**

BAND NERDS
Bonus Content

More quotes from **The 13th Chair**

Written By
DJ Corchin

Illustrated By
Dan Dougherty

The phazelFOZ Company, LLC

We need to bring people together to save music programs.
Let's limit it to one oboe player per group though.

    It doesn't matter where in the world you're from, you'll still have to explain what a euphonium is.

The magic of the band room is when you graduate,
it looks different for everyone.

    You say you support music education, but I do not think it means what you think it means.

Music education is not something to be taken lightly. It's not an afterthought. It's not a nice-to-do. It's essential to the well-being of the human race and we are ignoring it.

    Sometimes I put so much into my music I lose weight.

You may never be 1st chair. You may never be drum major.
You may never be in the top band.
But you will be a leader of a generation that will help shape
the world.
That is music's promise.

    There are no chair placements when it comes to people.

"You guys should wear stormtrooper helmets during marching band. That would be cool."
"How would we play our clarinets?"
"Exactly."

If the world embraced music education, there would be no more war. Except between the flutes.

Start a flute recital by drawing it out from behind your back like a barbarian sword. Pretty sure you'll have the audience's attention.

Easter: What a euphonium player calls their only gig.

No the two of us are not playing this duet too aggressively. It's how we make up.

There's too much good at stake to not practice.

Proof French Horn players are the intellectual sneaky type of rebellious: they designed their instrument to be played with their left hand. Feel their sassy wrath.

People in band, please run for office when you're older and fix all this.

If instruments had personalities the sax would be thoughtful. It comes to YOU.

Something is happening. Everyonem is having the same dream. No one remembers it they just wake up saying, "We have a fine selection of tuners and cheeses."

**If I'm going to fight for music education,
I want an awesome fighter name.**

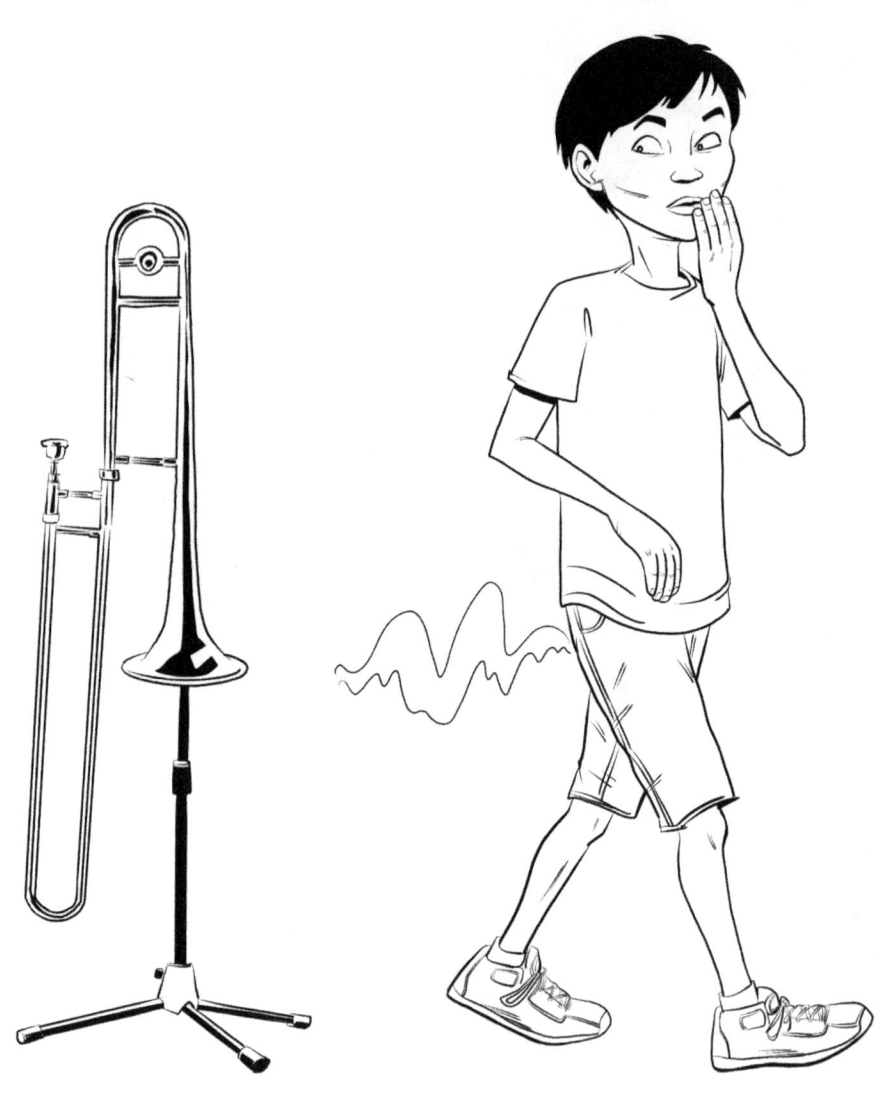

You reach a new level in your relationship when you fart in front of your instrument.

In case no one gets it from my playing, I put a globe under my chair so people know my music puts me on top of the world.

Managing all your relationships in band is like
managing all your social media accounts.
You gotta keep them all updated.

Egotistical lead trumpets are like pimples in your ear.
You want to get rid of them but you know it would hurt like hell.

Anyone planning on giving birth should take oboe lessons.

I don't just make music, I make you feel things. Deep down in your intestines, second star to the right, I'm gonna create a dancing GIF, that love that got away, things.

Am I the only one that dreams of putting a small marble
in a French horn as a part of a giant Rube Goldberg machine?

Music creates beautiful things around it wherever it goes.
It is at its core, love.

Sometimes I wonder why more boogers don't come
out while people are playing. Science is crazy yo.

If I were king I'd wear a humble crown of eighth notes...
made of 24 karat gold, lined in blue sapphires & yellow
diamonds, & forged by blacksmith band directors.
'Cause I be king yo.

Ironically it's easy to say you're a tough politician because you can make the tough cuts. 'Cause clearly adding music to education has been super easy.

I'm not out of tune. Update your app.

When I say I love this piece I mean I have solo in it.

I don't know how to connect with another human being but good thing I scored high on my tests. Was worried I might not be successful there for a minute.

The light should always be on in the band room.

The day you go to try out instruments is like the day you put on the sorting hat.

I feel like band is a righty and orchestra's a lefty.

Playing an instrument needs to be on everyone's bucket list. Don't get outta here without experiencing that.

**My instrument doesn't need to say it loves me,
I know by how it plays for me.
Maybe someone should take the hint?**

Sometimes I play softly by the fire with no other lights on, but then I realize I'm alone and that's weird.

When people ask, "If you were stranded on a desert island what would you bring?" I answer, an audience.

Practicing IS sexy. Bow chicka wow wow.

> You can love your music. Just don't be the clingy, I need attention all the time, celebrate an anniversary each week, talk about it to everyone you know, if you loved me you'd know what to do person in the relationship.

When we listen to each other we get better.
One thing you wouldn't hear is standardized tests.

> The single biggest problem in today's political landscape is not just that we think we're right, but that everyone else is wrong. Could you imagine how terrible music would be if we all did that?

I once asked a French horn player out. They sarcastically laughed and walked away without answering. Pretty sure that means yes in French Horn.

> Happy Valentine's Day. When music people celebrate their true second love.

Music has a voice. It sounds like you. Speak up.

Sometimes I put a trumpet up to my lips, scrunch my face and move my fingers real fast like I'm killing it.

**All mythical creatures play a mythical instrument.
My unicorn plays the euphonium.**

I pre-licked your reed for you. Pay it forward.

If you know the difference between a baritone and euphonium you're awesome. If you know the difference between what makes one conical and one cylindrical you're a badass. This is all assuming you have tattoos, go rock climbing without a harness, and eat raw meat as a snack.

>If I were a teeny tiny person I would live on a French horn because it would look like a super futuristic city.

When you need to make music but you can't. Those are worst days of all.

>When the piece ends, I may stop being in love with you. Music does that to me.

If the band were a burger, I feel like the saxes would be the mayo. You know it's there and it's too hard to scrape off so you go ahead and eat it anyways. But then you're like "hey, I kinda like mayo on my burger now."

>My soul is just as dynamic as my music. Which is why I get yelled at on numerous levels.

If you put a mirror on your stand and angle it just right you can shine a bright light in the eyes of your nemesis. And yes, you have a nemesis.

My life is like music. At first I enjoy all the loud and crazy parts.
Then I learn to appreciate the soft, delicate intricacies.

Sometimes I record myself and when I play it back for
someone I say it's a famous player. Then watch their
expression.

Band is like hot chocolate. It's warm and sweet
and sometimes burns like hell. But then you take
another sip.

You shoved a sock in your instrument and tried to blow it out.
Now your lips smell like feet. Correction, MORE like feet.

Bb Major Scale. Comfort food for band people.

I sprinkle music on my vegetables. They taste better.

Did you ever get the funny feeling someone's
looking at you during rehearsal and then you look
up and it's the director?

The cool thing about the voices in my head is that they all play different instruments.

If I were asked by aliens who they should take if they wanted to start an ideal human colony on their world, I would say visit the band rooms. If I were asked by aliens.

I'm so psyched for the competition I woke up in full uniform.

How did someone invent the bassoon? Like they sat around one day and said, yeah let's try that.

If music hasn't taught you to be kind, you're doing it wrong.

If your director uses the words "hashtag taking it to the next level," your music education probably isn't all that it could be.

My instrument has GPS tracking on me so if I'm ever lost, music can find me.

For the holidays all I want is a bill passed that creates more jobs, better education, healthier people, and less conflict in the world. We'll call it Music Education Appropriations Bill 101.

When you're amazing at oboe but your director won't let you play unless it's bassoon. Let it go. Let it go. And then freeze their face.

Sometimes when I put away a clarinet I grab it with both hands and pull it apart pretending I'm the Hulk. Then I gently place it in it's case and cover it with a soft cloth. You know, 'cause it's expensive.

Only playing in keys that have sharps is like being a band vegan.

If band were fruit, baritones would be kiwi. A little fuzzy on the outside, kinda messy but generally ok when you see underneath.

A cell phone ring only ruins the moment if you let it.

I practice with the lights off because when I'm playing, I can see in the darkness.

Flutes are just lightsaber hilts. If I had to guess, they're red blades.

I knew I loved you when during band I thought about you and during you, I thought about band...and maybe a cheeseburger.

The audience will hear what you want them to hear when you play the arrangement you want to play, subtly bringing out the parts you choose, to shape the presentation of the piece. Kind of like what we teach our children. Let them hear it all.

Be ok with dissonance, work toward resolution.

Sometimes I pretend the keys on a sax are little mouths talking. They say really inappropriate things.

I think sharps are really hashtags describing my life.

                        I'm so band I can do tremolo on Slurpee machine.

Think about the words we use to describe how we evaluate our students, "standardized," "common." Nothing meaningful has ever come from those words. Music forward.

                        If life is a late night, music is my coffee.

Music education has done so much for you, what have you done for it? I mean at least send it a card or something.

        Can we please have uniforms that turn us invisible for general effect? We promise to only use them for good...mostly.

In music even the smallest part has significance. In politics significance is the smallest part.

                You know I love you when I practice in front of you. Or I just didn't know you were there. Could be either.

Whole notes are the healthiest type of notes. Nom nom nom.

Sharps even look uncomfortable.

> Sometimes I play a really high note and am like, "come at me bro." Then I realize I'm just playing an instrument and probably shouldn't have spoken like that.

I order my food with musical expressions.
I like my steak cooked con brio.

> Funny how all my GPS apps lead to the band room.

In all the eons of music evolution one thing has remained the same since the dawn of time, the miscellaneous percussion drawer.

> Every part of me is musical. I mean EVERY part.

If you're learning music you're learning to innovate.

> Why take half steps when you can take whole steps?

If you make band about winning, in the long run you always lose. If you make it about excellence you can never fail.

I once said that flutes play with too much vibrato. Once.

Every band should have a pet plant. They can grow together and supply each other with their expelled gasses.

> I tried to carve a French horn into my pumpkin. It did not go well. The pumpkin got all attitud-y

The thing about band is that you tend to only remember the great performances. If we could only do that in life we'd all be a little less stressed.

> I think we should get multiple choices of D.S. Symbols. Kinda like a choose your own adventure.

Making music allows me to make other things. Like peace with myself and friends.

> I'm putting identical twins on opposite ends of the field and then act like they're one person marching really fast.

Just because I'm thinking about the passthrough at letter C, my horn angle for the snake formation, the follow the leader before the "blow your face off" feature, and the hip switch at 208 BPM doesn't mean I don't think about you. It just means I think about you less.

I'm bringing a trombone with me wherever I go. That way if someone is invading my personal space I'm prepared.

I want to build a second marching field above the current marching field. That way we can take our show to the next level.

> So relieved to know the light at the end of the tunnel is a marching band field.

Nothing better than falling asleep on your friend's shoulder during a quiet late night bus ride home after a great show. Except maybe driving home instead in your brand new Audi you happen to win at a random raffle you entered by accident because you thought you were putting your name in for a free piece of pizza at the concession stand. But you also get the free pizza. Yeah that would be better.

> If you truly love me you will have nachos waiting for me when I'm off the field.

Cold nights during competitions I tend to hang by the trumpets. You know, all the hot air.

> We're not moving around "emotionally" while we're playing. We're air-writing messages to each other.

If you bully someone, I don't care how well you play, you're not a musician.

> Anyone else think it's weird people are still quiet in a music library?

I only love two things. My music and ice cream.
Thought I was going to say you didn't you?
Nope, music and ice cream.

I now use a drone to mark my parts.

Forget cookies, when Santa came down the chimney I gave him the gift of music and blew a high F in his face.

The time between walking into the band room and
when the tuning note is played is sacred.

        Tubas are like armpits. Used to make fart sounds.

Sometimes we get scored lower than we deserve. Clearly judges error. When we get scored higher though, the judge clearly saw something inspiring deep within us that even we didn't see. Judges are amazing.

        Our plumes are like Swiffers except they pick up Awesome particles. Still get just as dirty though.

You make me smile then I go sharp.

        A sax kind of looks like it started as a clarinet transformer but half way through they were like, "naw this is too hard," then it got stuck that way.

Good thing I backed up my old instrument before I updated to my new bigger instrument.

        A section leader who thinks they're the best is like Decaf Coffee. Ineffective.

The nub on the bottom of a slide is there to get right in between your big and middle toe. So nice.

I pretend the snare stand is a giant grab-o-hand and use it to try and pick up stuff.

I'm so band I do bicep curls with a tuba...player.

Music should have just the right amount of silliness in it.

There's something different about school during 6am rehearsals. I think it's the smell.

Music is a doorway to do big things. Do big things.

Don't tell me you support music and only pay for it when there's an open case on the ground.

I feel like if sections were sandwiches the horns would have a lot of avocado and fancy mustard on them.

If Guard used lightsabers instead of regular sabers the anxiety you feel during a toss would be on a whole other level.

Standardized testing is like coaching every player on every team the same way. Suddenly that's crazy.

I'm like the Robin Hood of my band. I take the trumpet's pencils and give them to those who will use them more.

Even if I'm practicing by myself in the band room, I'm never really alone. You know...the ghost.

We all show courage differently. I do it by picking up timpani by the rim in front of the percussion section.

**Sometimes I feel the urge to straighten a bocal.
Bocal: the band's paperclip.**

I don't play my instrument. I work my instrument.

        Without moms band wouldn't exist. And if they did exist, they would look terrible.

You know when you can't always tell when something is there, but you definitely feel it when it's not? Oboes are not that.

        Musicians should have the title "Cardiologist" on their business card.

With all the advances in technology, we still don't have retractable podiums. No more tripping, just...rise.

        When I smile from across the section it's because I know the audition results before you do.

You can't move your band forward hiring movers. Get yourself a rental truck and good friends dedicated to making it happen with the promise of cheap pizza. You don't want strangers touch'n your stuff.

        You may be passionate but you're also out of tune.

Music is a non-contact art form. Unless you insult my art form. Then prepare to be contacted.

I believe in practice so much I practice breaking my own heart. You know... in case.

Someone once described an embouchure as kissing your instrument. I wouldn't recommend kissing anyone like that.

We have a national doughnut day but no national music education day? Listen, I'm cool with combining the two.

Music is about sharing, even if it's with yourself. Don't be stingy.

Bassoon concertos are like Brussel sprouts. As a kid you're like no way. As an adult you kinda like'm but only roasted and covered in seasoning.

We should change August to March. It just seems appropriate.

It's sad that when we see a female director we think, "That's cool." Playing music from the past is cool. Living in it is not. Still got a long way to go.

Sometimes I speak in 7/8 and people think I have the hiccups.

I hope you don't mean "I love you" the way you mean "I practiced."

Sometimes I practice in the bathroom. Things take a little longer, ya know, 'cause of all the extra fermatas.

**Trombones are like onions. Onions are like ogres.
Trombones are like ogres.**

I'm a musician so when you say "that's music to my ears" you can understand why I might think you're exaggerating.

>Music is totally one of those things worth getting up early for. It goes Pancakes, Music, Christmas. In that order.

Music is like butter on my toast. It melts all over me and gets in my crevices.

>I might be lost in my music, but I'm never lost with my music.

Good music is like a good dad. Kicks your butt to help you get better and makes you feel like you can accomplish anything.

>The only time I put down my phone is to pick up my instrument. I'm ok with that.

If you can move a phrase you can move a mountain.

>If you can dodge a wrench you can dodge the evil French horn death stare.

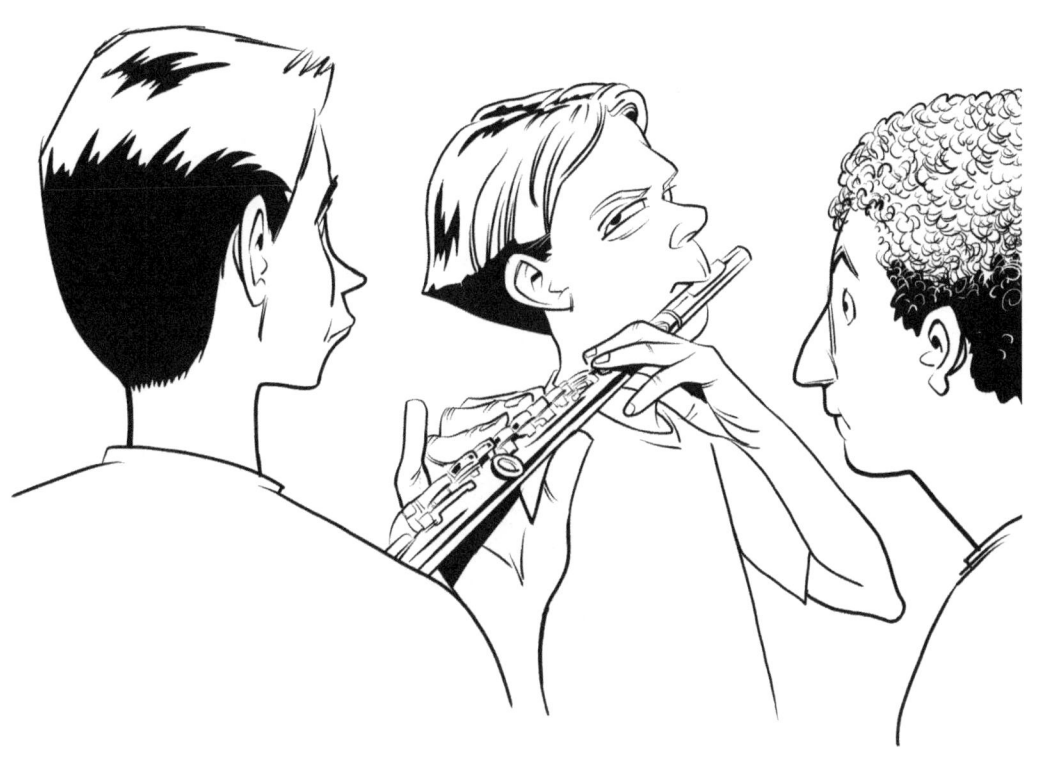

When a tuba player squints it's because their stand is too far away to see the music. When a flute player squints, they're thinking about putting a dead fish in your instrument locker.

Diversity isn't a word. It's an action. If you're not there yet with your band you haven't DONE enough.

> Band camp is like everyone going to the pool together. At first a bit awkward but then you realize everyone is in their swimsuits too. Then you're cool.

When I fall asleep in band it's because I like the music in my head better.

> Those aren't quarter notes oboes, they're sound waves.

July 4th we get to play my favorite instrument... the cannon. Not because it's fun, but because we turn an instrument of war into an instrument of music. But I do really like the bang it makes.

> I listen to everyone who tells me "you can't do that." Then I take the sounds they make and arrange them for wind ensemble. I'm amazing that way.

When a baby is feeling sad, alone, and not sure what to do in life we sing to it. We don't do trigonometry with them. But let's keep cutting music.

If band were a fish tank, tubas would be like that sucker fish thing that hangs out in the back.

Sometimes I think I have a solo then realize the part is doubled somewhere else. Pretty sure that person will have car trouble on concert night.

Silly that adding just one vertical line to a test bubble makes it go from meaningless to life changing.

The End...
Or is it?
Yeah it is.
For now.
Until the next book comes out.
Probably next year.
But ya never know.
I might be out of ideas.
No! I must go on.
I must continue the good fight.
People depend on me.
I'm like the Band Nerd Batman.
Yes, I am Batman.
Who's my Robin?
Probably an Alto Sax Player.
It just seems like Robin would play Alto.
Man I'm hungry.
I could go for some sushi.
Batman eats sushi right?
How good is sushi?
So good.

All quotes are original. Any resemblance to other quotes is strictly coincidental. Those other quotes are probably the lame version of these though.

The 13th Chair